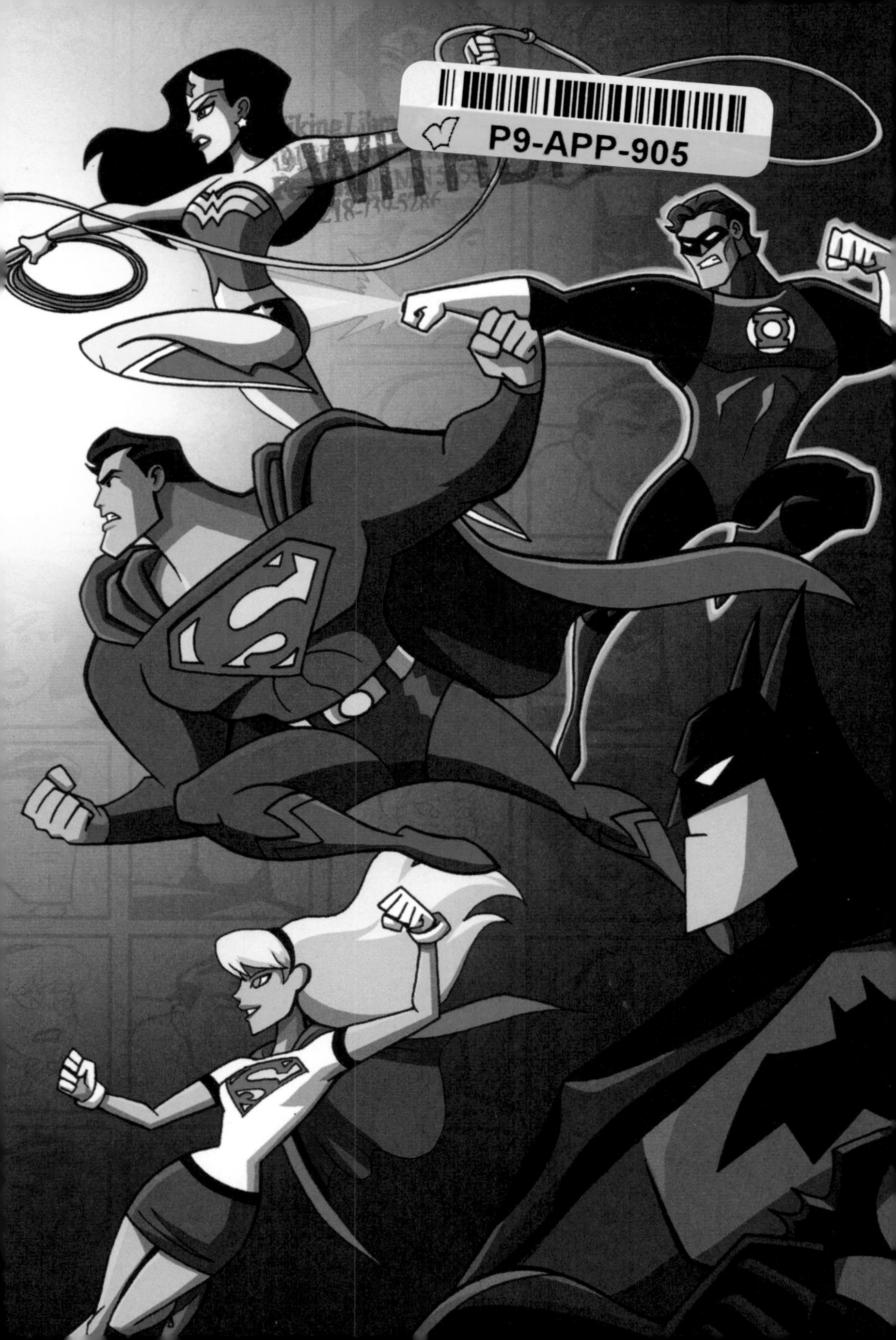

SUPERGIRL™ vs. BRAINIAC

WRITTEN BY
SCOTT SONNEBORN

ILLUSTRATED BY
LUCIANO VECCHIO

SUPERGIRL BASED ON
THE CHARACTERS CREATED BY
JERRY SIEGEL AND JOE SHUSTER
BY SPECIAL ARRANGEMENT WITH
THE JERRY SIEGEL FAMILY

STONE ARCH BOOKS
a capstone imprint

Published by Stone Arch Books in 2013
A Capstone Imprint
1710 Roe Crest Drive
North Mankato, MN 56003
www.capstonepub.com

Copyright © 2013 DC Comics.
SUPERGIRL and all related characters and elements are
trademarks of and © DC Comics.
(s13)

STAR29361

No part of this publication may be reproduced in whole
or in part, or stored in a retrieval system, or transmitted
in any form or by any means, electronic, mechanical,
photocopying, recording, or otherwise, without written
permission.

Cataloging-in-Publication Data is available at the Library
of Congress website
ISBN: 978-1-4342-6015-4 (library binding)

Summary: Earth is under attack by a billion Brainiacs!
The evil android and his cold and calculating clones have
tricked Superman into straying far from Earth, leaving
the planet ripe for the picking. Only Supergirl stands a
chance of shutting down the super-villain's army.

Designed by Hilary Wacholz

Printed in the United States of America in Stevens Point, Wisconsin.
032013   007227WZF13

TABLE OF CONTENTS

CHAPTER 1
INVASION 6

CHAPTER 2
SUPERGIRL VS. BRAINIACS! 12

CHAPTER 3
THE MIND OF A TEENAGER 19

CHAPTER 4
BRAINIAC VS. BRAINIAC 32

CHAPTER 5
BLOWN AWAY 43

SUPERGIRL™

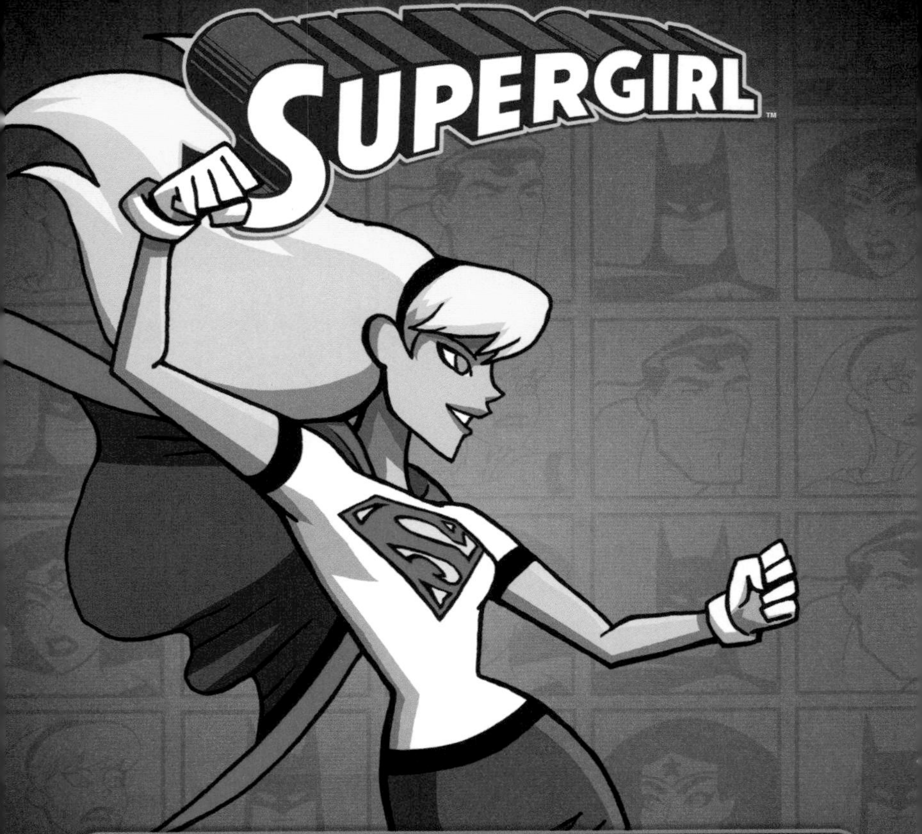

REAL NAME: Kara Zor-El (Kent)

ROLE: Super hero

BASE: Metropolis

ABILITIES: Supergirl is from the planet Krypton. She has all the powers and abilities of her cousin, Superman, including invulnerability, flight, super-strength, and super-speed. Like all Kryptonians, Supergirl is vulnerable to Kryptonite.

BRAINIAC

REAL NAME: Unknown

ROLE: Super-villain

BASE: Mobile

ABILITIES: Brainiac was Krypton's supercomputer before he destroyed the planet. He has a genius-level intellect and can take control of most forms of technology. He also has super-strength and the power of flight.

CHAPTER 1

INVASION

As the sun rose over Metropolis, the city was already alive with activity. Cars honked as they fought their way through midtown traffic. People rushed across the sidewalks on their way to work.

Then suddenly everything came to a standstill. Everyone on the street looked up as something clouded the bright sky. **WHOOOSH!** Brainiac zoomed down toward Metropolis. Using the factories on planet Linsnar, he had built a powerful, new robotic body for himself.

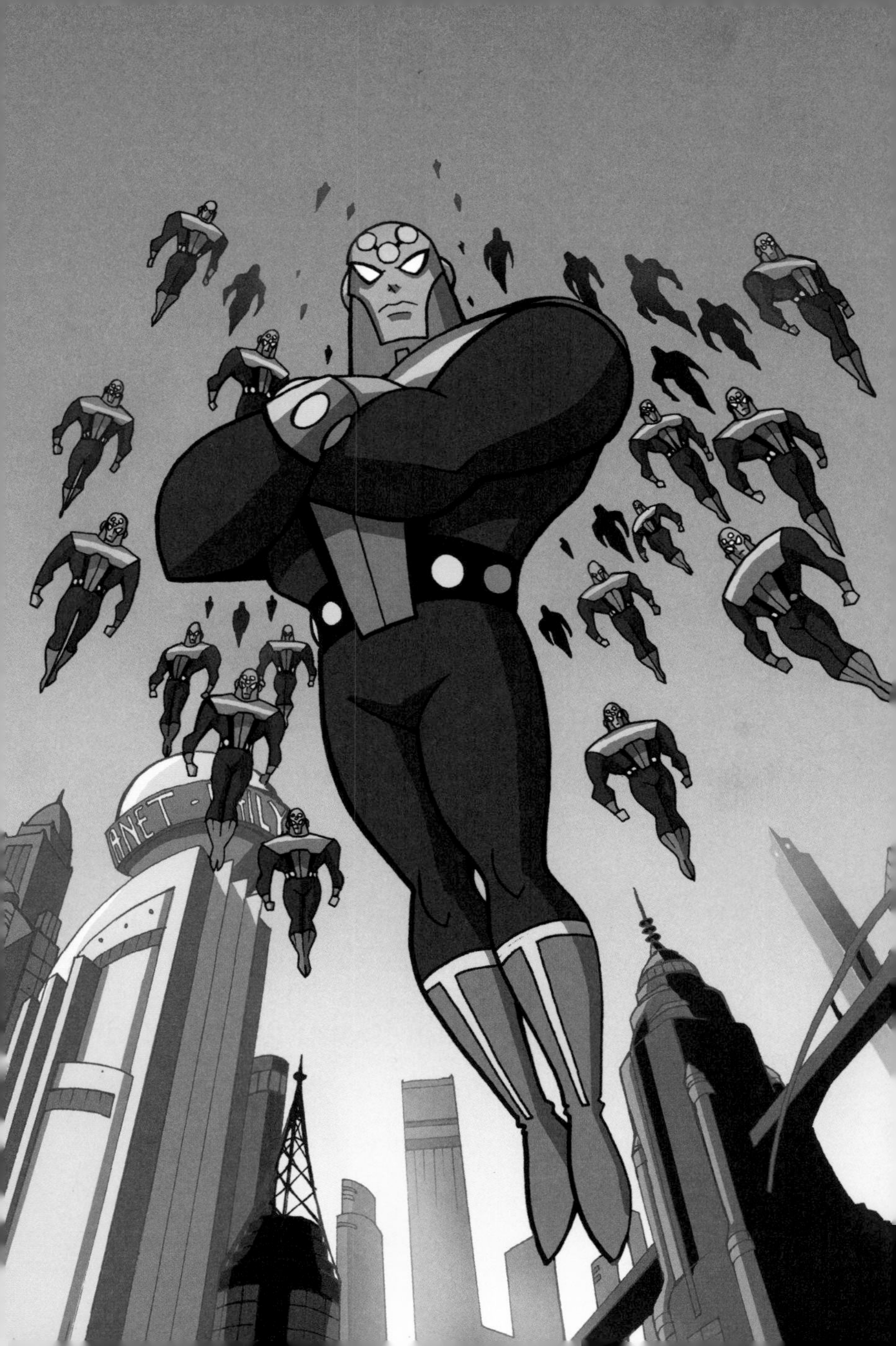

But that wasn't the only thing he had used the factories to create. **WHOOSH!** Behind Brainiac flew a dozen identical robot copies of himself.

"What's happening?" cried a man on the street. "I thought there was only one Brainiac!"

"You are correct," said Brainiac. "I am the only Brainiac. These robotic copies are identical to me in every way except for one — they are mindless drones who obey my every command. And my first command is for them to attack!"

Everyone on the street fled as the robots zoomed down and attacked the city.

The people knew that Brainiac had tried to invade Earth several times before. He always failed. The reason was always the same: Superman stopped him.

But this time, Brainiac was sure he would succeed. Before he departed from the planet Linsnar, Brainiac activated a distress signal and left it running. Brainiac knew that Superman would respond to Linsnar's distress call as soon as he received it.

With Superman millions of miles away from Earth, there was no chance he could return before Brainiac completed his work.

"I will harvest every byte of data that Earth possesses," Brainiac announced to the citizens of Metropolis. "I will start with this city, Metropolis. When I am finished, I will delete this world. And this time, Superman is not here to save you. This time, I have thought of everything."

"Well, except for one thing," said a voice. "Me!"

Brainiac turned to see a teenaged girl flying in the sky. She wore a bright red cape with a yellow S-shield on it.

"I don't think we've met," she said with a smile. "I'm Supergirl!"

WHAM! She struck Brainiac with all her might. Her slender fist tore through Brainiac's metallic skin.

Supergirl grabbed hold of whatever circuits and wires she found inside and pulled.

CRUNCH! Brainiac burst open. The tiny pieces of his metal body sprinkled down over the street like a light snow.

Supergirl shrugged. "I guess he's not all that hard to defeat," she said.

"You are incorrect," said a voice, seemingly from thin air.

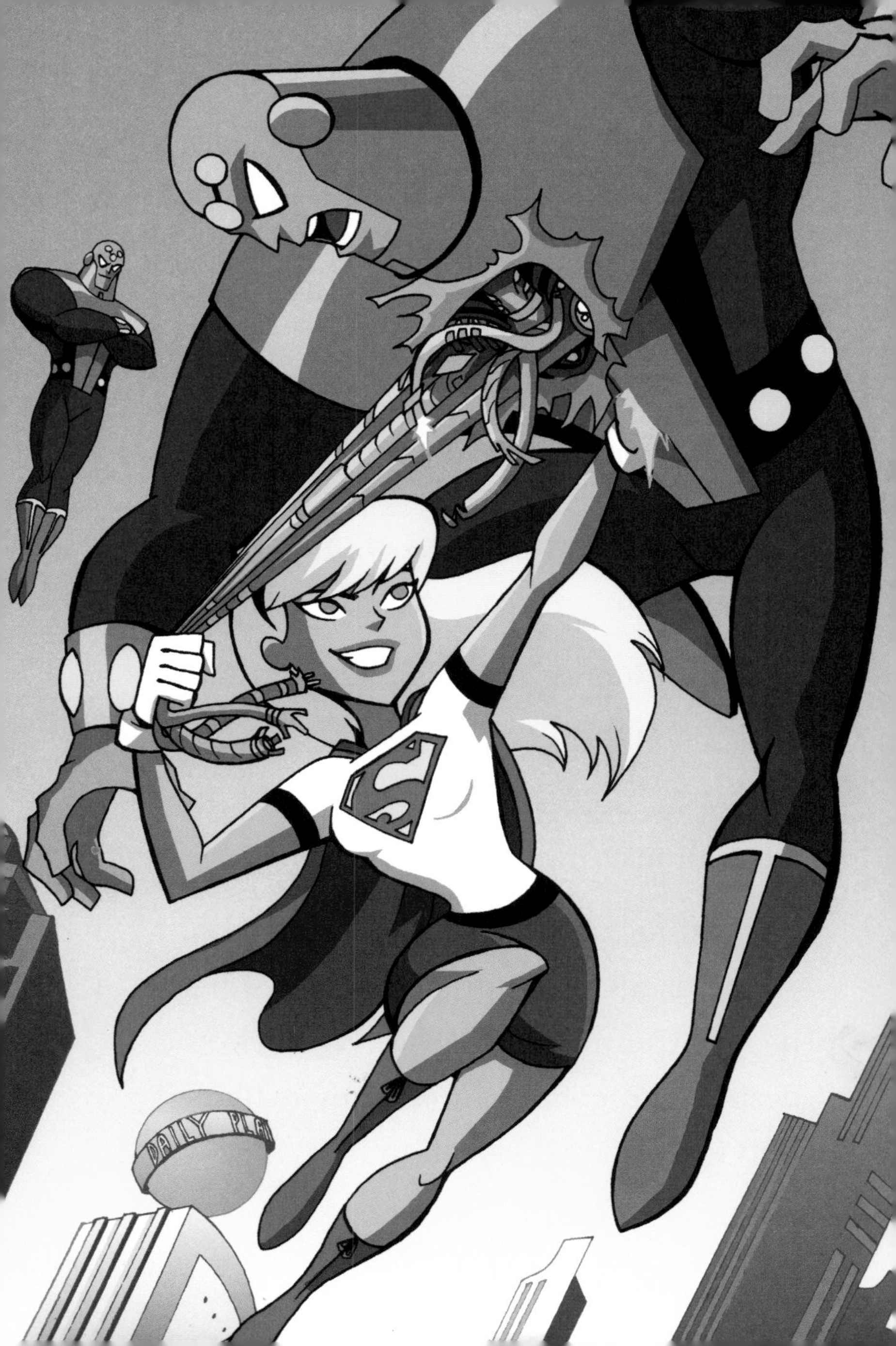
DAILY

CHAPTER 2

SUPERGIRL VS. BRAINIACS!

Supergirl saw the eyes of one of Brainiac's robotic copies turn a fierce red.

"Hello again," said the new Brainiac as he came online.

"Wait!" said Supergirl. "You said these were all just 'mindless robot copies.'"

Brainiac grinned coldly. "Each robot copy has all of my programming stored deep within it," he replied. "When you destroyed me, the nearest copy activated, and I transferred myself to it."

Supergirl sighed. "So let me guess," she said. "I'll have to smash all these robots if I want to get rid of you."

"That is correct," said Brainiac. "You have little chance of accomplishing that."

SHOOOMP! A panel opened up on Brainiac's chest. **FWISH!** Thick ropes of metal shot out from his body. They wrapped around Supergirl and pulled tight.

"UNGH!" cried Supergirl. Brainiac's metal tentacles bit into her skin.

Supergirl flexed her arms. **CRACK!** The tentacles broke apart. Then she flew right into Brainiac and knocked him backward with a **THUD!**

KA-BLAM! She kicked hard, sending him tumbling through the air. Brainiac stopped himself from spiraling upward without the slightest effort.

"Impressive," Brainiac said, turning to face Supergirl. "But I expect no less from a Kryptonian."

Supergirl's eyes went wide.

"Yes, I have surmised that you are from Krypton," Brainiac said, predicting her thoughts. "I observed your super-strength and the markings on your costume. You are from the same place as Superman."

Supergirl rolled her eyes. "Wow, did you figure that out all by yourself?" she scoffed.

"Yes," said Brainiac. "I just said I did."

"Yeah, duh!" said Supergirl. "I was making fun of you. Man, you're even more lame than my algebra teacher."

Brainiac extended his fists. **_FOOM!_** **_FOOM!_** They shot out from their sockets toward Supergirl.

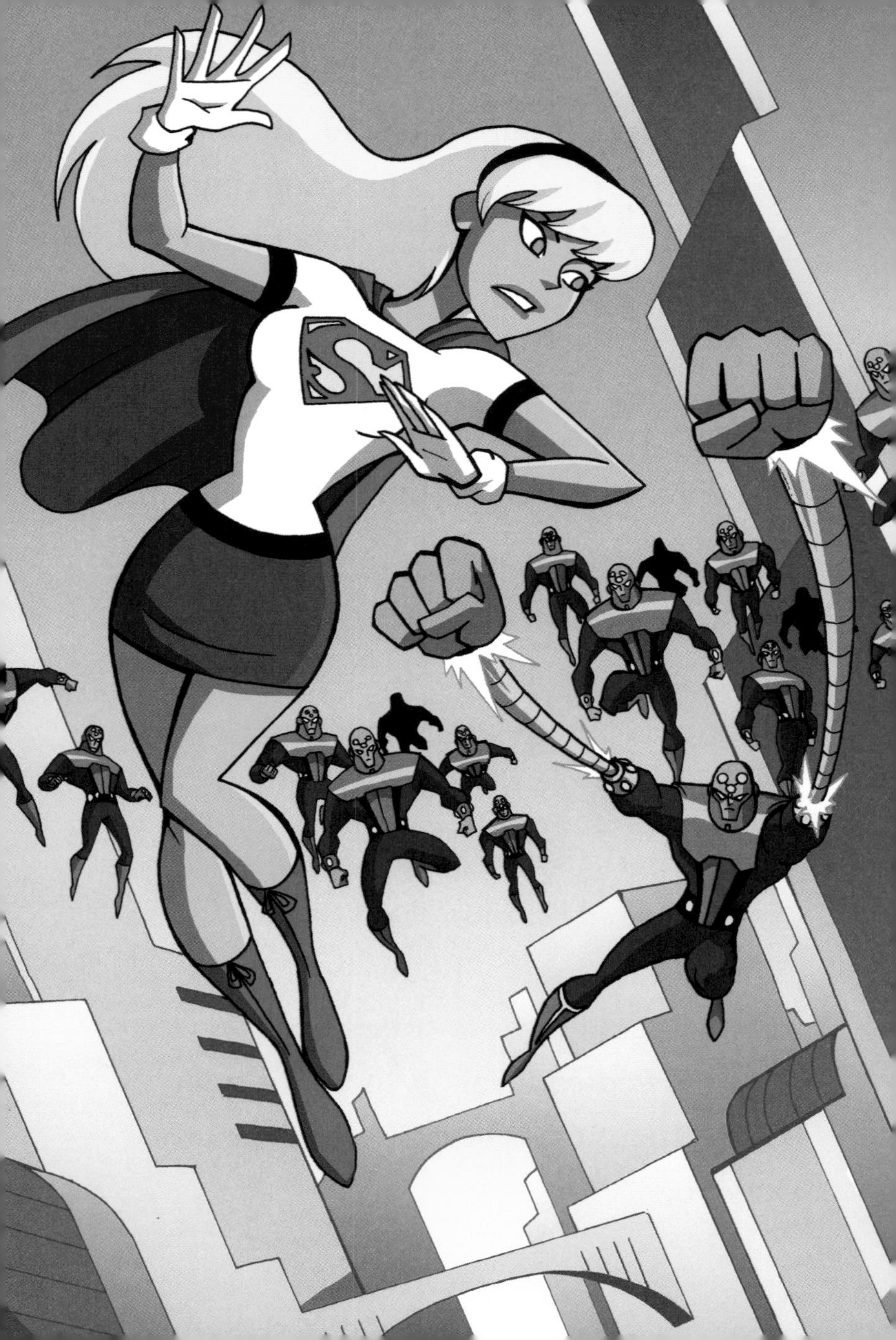

"Hands off!" Supergirl said. **WHAM!** **BAM!** She punched his fists right back at him. **CLINK!** **CLANK!** They reattached to Brainiac's arms.

"I'm not so sure you're as smart as you think you are," Supergirl said.

"I assure you that I am," said Brainiac.

"You said Superman and I came from the same place," said Supergirl. "Well, I'm from Argo City. My home escaped from Krypton before the planet was destroyed. So I'm from a different place than he is."

Brainiac stood very still as his computerized brain processed what Supergirl had said. "I have heard of Argo City," he said as he scanned his memory files. "It floated through space for many years. Then it was lost. There were no survivors."

"There was one," Supergirl said proudly. "And she's about to pound your face in!"

Brainiac's metal tentacles snaked out of his chest and grabbed Supergirl. She struggled, but Brainiac held her tight.

"Then you possess data I do not have," said Brainiac. "Data I can now get only from Argo City's sole survivor — you!"

"Not going to happen," said Supergirl.

CRACK! Supergirl broke free of the powerful tentacles and then flew right at Brainiac. He simply opened his mouth and released a tiny nanobot copy of himself.

FWA-ZAP! Supergirl blasted the large Brainiac with her heat vision. He instantly melted into a pile of liquid-metal sludge. As Brainiac's body melted, his nanobot copy floated through Supergirl's mouth and into her body.

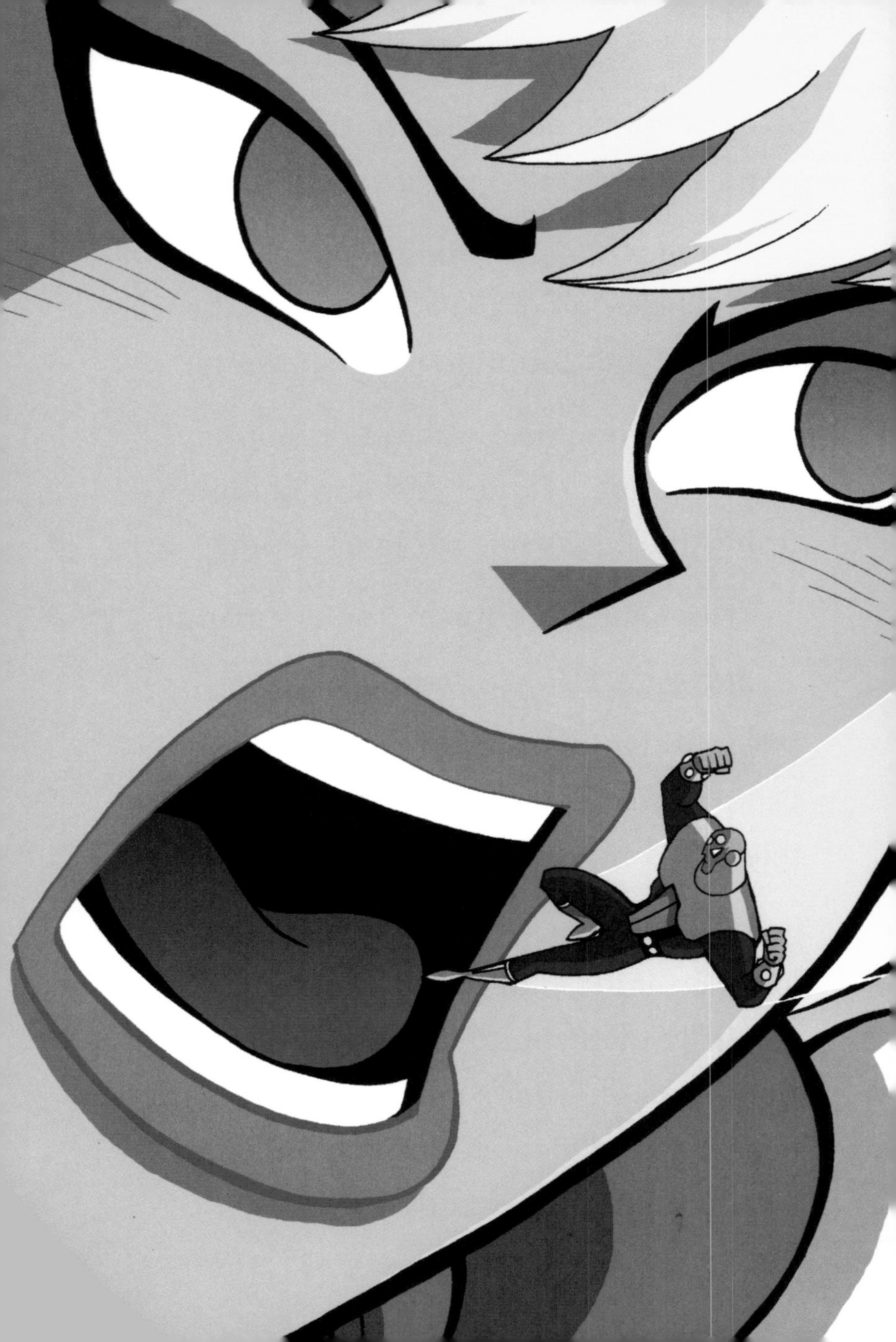

CHAPTER 3

THE MIND OF A TEENAGER

SWOOSH! The miniature Brainiac flew faster and faster. Soon he reached his destination — Supergirl's brain! From his microscopic point of view, her brain looked like a forest of floating trees. The "trees" were actually many, many neurons. According to Brainiac's calculations, there were about 100 billion of them.

Each neuron had dozens of skinny branches dangling from it. The branches reached toward other neurons, but they did not touch.

Thoughts, memories, and ideas passed from one neuron to the next. They blasted across the gaps in electrical bursts. **FZZT!** **FZZT!** Brainiac dodged them, zooming toward a specific part of Supergirl's brain.

"The memories that are recalled most often are stored here," Brainiac said to himself. "Surely, this is where I will find Supergirl's memories of Argo City."

FWAZAAAP! An electrical burst leaped from one nearby neuron to another. That bit of electricity was part of a memory making its way through Supergirl's brain.

Even though he was barely larger than a molecule, Brainiac knew his body could absorb dozens of electrical blasts like that one. It would take hundreds of blasts — maybe even thousands — firing all at once to harm him.

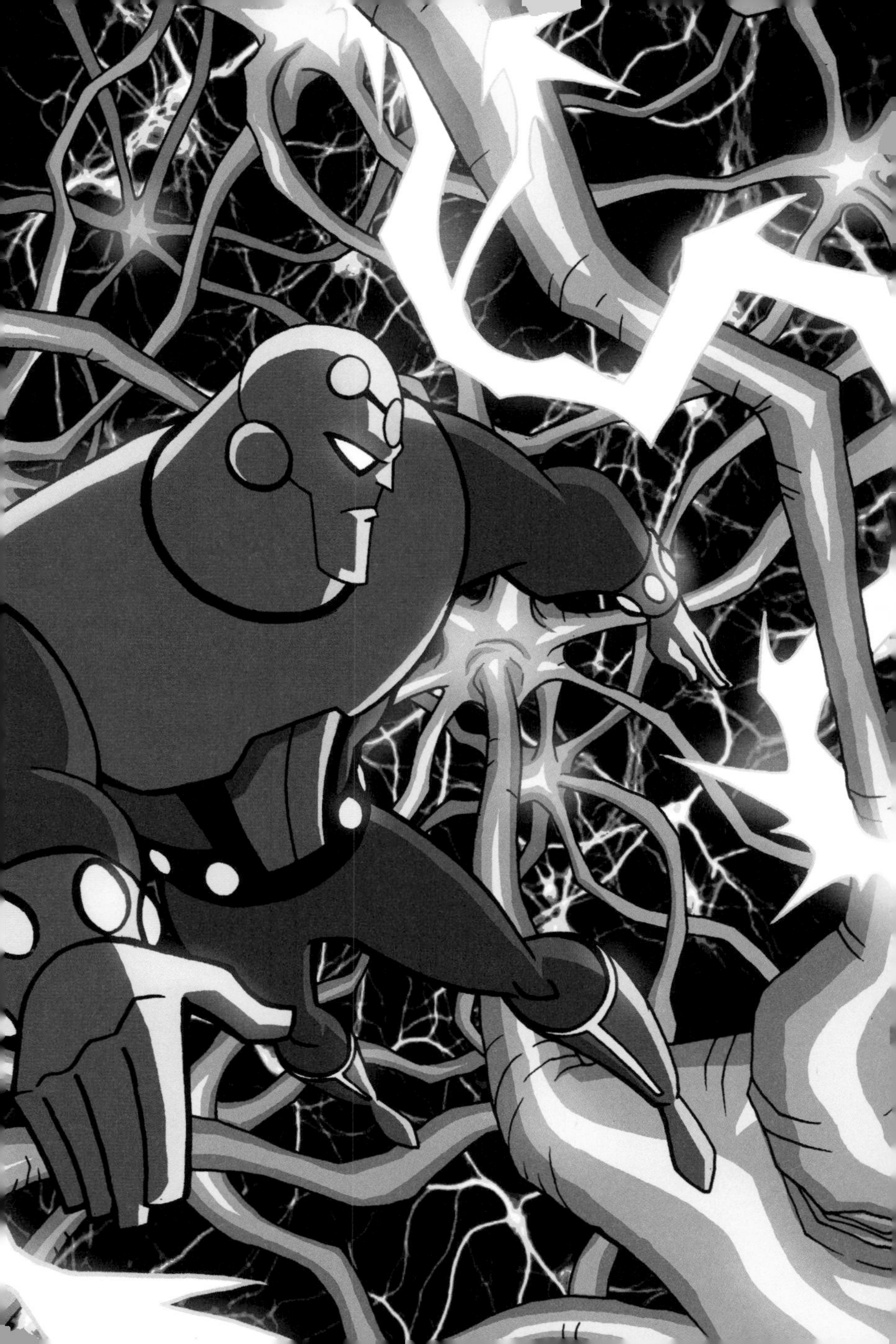

Brainiac positioned himself between two neurons. **FWAAAZAP!** An electrical burst shot out of one of the neurons. Before it could reach the other neuron, Brainiac absorbed it.

The electrical burst contained a memory. **WHIRRRR!** Brainiac's computer processors studied the memory. It was about someone named Captain Joey. *Perhaps he was an important military leader in Argo City*, thought Brainiac. *I need more information.*

"Supergirl!" Brainiac shouted.

"Who said that?" asked Supergirl.

"It is I, Brainiac," said the tiny villain. "I am inside your mind."

"What?!" replied Supergirl. "Get out of there, you creep!"

"No," replied Brainiac. "I will not leave until I have taken every memory you possess of Argo City. Now tell me, who is Captain Joey?"

FWZAAAP!

Another electrical burst of memory blasted out of a nearby neuron. Brainiac absorbed that memory as well.

"And what is . . . the Park Ridge Mall?" he asked as he scanned the new memory. "Was it some kind of military facility in Argo City?"

"You've got to be kidding me," said Supergirl. "Park Ridge Mall is the best place to shop in all of Metropolis."

"Surely Captain Joey was an important leader in Argo City," said Brainiac. "What position did he hold?"

"You're telling me you don't know who Captain Joey is?" Supergirl asked. "Every kid in Metropolis grew up listening to his song 'Hob's Bay Hairspray!'"

FWAZAP! *FWAZAP!* **FWAZAP!** Neurons fired all around Brainiac as Supergirl remembered the song. Brainiac quickly moved out of the way to avoid being overloaded by so many electrical blasts.

"I do not understand," replied Brainiac. "How could the place in your mind that should hold the information you find most important be full of data about insipid songs and shopping complexes?"

Supergirl shrugged. "It's what I like."

WHAM! Supergirl was suddenly slammed down to the ground. She hit the concrete sidewalk with a *CRUNCH!*

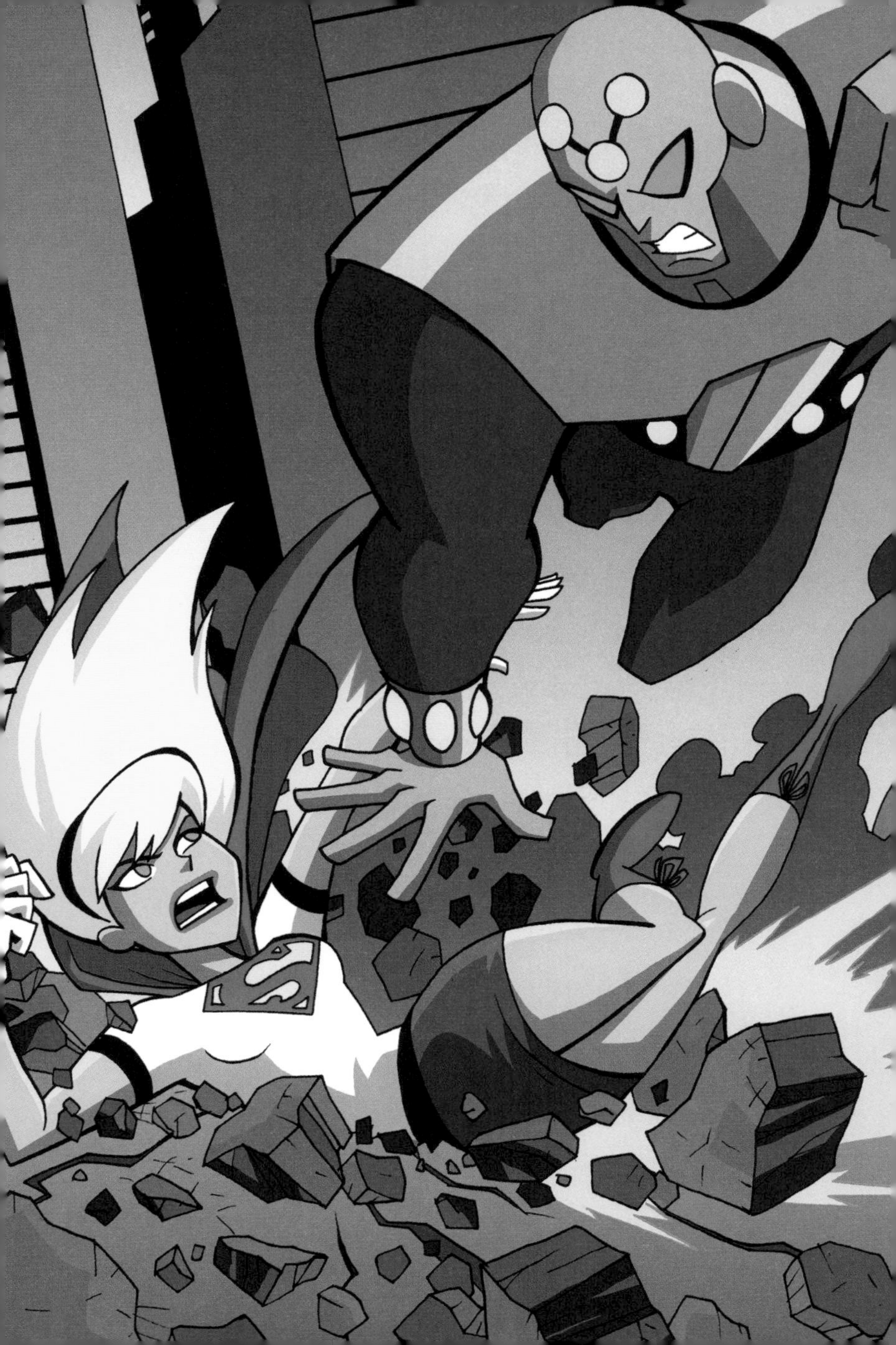

Supergirl picked herself up. Behind her stood one of the robotic copies of Brainiac. This one was different from the others, though. Its eyes shined a sinister red.

"I am Brainiac," it said.

"What?" said a very confused Supergirl. "I thought Brainiac was in my head."

"When you destroyed my robotic body," said Brainiac from inside her brain, "the nearest copy followed its pre-coded instructions and activated its programming. It did not know that I had survived inside your brain. So it became me."

"So now there are two of you?" exclaimed Supergirl. "That's way too much jerkiness for one city."

"I am unfamiliar with the word 'jerkiness,'" replied Brainiac.

"Well, look it up on the Internet," said Supergirl. "I'm sure you'll find a picture of you next to the definition."

WHIRRRRRR!

Brainiac's computer processors hummed to life. "I just looked up the definition on the Internet," he said. "I did not find a picture of myself there."

"Wonderful," groaned Supergirl. "I get a villain stuck in my head, and it turns out it doesn't even understand sarcasm."

FWISSSH! The Brainiac standing on the street shot a metallic fist at Supergirl. **BAM!** It hit her — hard. She staggered back. **ZAP!** Supergirl blasted Brainiac with her heat vision.

"Stop," ordered the Brainiac in her brain. "You are fighting me out there."

"Just because you're shouting inside my head doesn't mean that I'm going to listen to you," replied Supergirl. "Besides, it's not like you can do anything to stop me from in there!"

"That is incorrect," Brainiac replied.

WHOOOSH!! Brainiac rocketed straight to her cerebrum. That part of the brain controlled Supergirl's body. He landed in between another set of neurons. As they fired off their electrical signals, Brainiac's metallic body intercepted and rerouted them.

Supergirl found herself turning to face the Brainiac that was hovering over the street. She tried to stop herself but couldn't.

"What's happening?!" Supergirl cried.

Then the Brainiac in her brain spoke through her mouth.

"It should be obvious," Brainiac said. "I am controlling your body and voice."

"Greetings, Brainiac," said the Brainiac floating above the street.

"To avoid confusion," said the Brainiac inside Supergirl's mind, "I will call you Brainiac Prime."

"I accept that designation," said the human-sized Brainiac, "even though you and I are identical copies of the same program."

"That is correct," replied Brainiac, using Supergirl's mouth.

"Okay, this is just weird!" said Supergirl. "Quit stealing my voice!"

"Please do not interrupt," said Brainiac, using her mouth. "Adults are talking."

"I concur," said Brainiac Prime.

"I have discovered that Supergirl is the only lifeform in the universe with knowledge of Argo City," said Brainiac.

"Then why have you not taken that knowledge from her and deleted her from existence?" asked Brainiac Prime.

"I have been attempting to do that," replied Brainiac. "Finding the knowledge is not so simple. Supergirl's brain is filled with useless information about human males, homework, kittens, and colorful clothing."

"Hey!" said Supergirl. "I didn't invite you inside my head! So it's pretty rude to insult what you found there."

Both Brainiacs ignored Supergirl.

"Still," Brainiac Prime told Brainiac, "you should have found the information you seek by now."

"You have never been inside a teenaged girl's mind," replied Brainiac. "You cannot possibly understand."

"Indeed," agreed Brainiac Prime. "I do not understand why it is taking so long. Therefore, I hypothesize that you must not be functioning properly. That must be what is causing this delay. A delay we cannot afford. This mission must be completed before Superman returns. Therefore, I give you this directive: delete Supergirl now, or be deleted with her!"

"No!" Brainiac shouted from Supergirl's mouth. "I must possess her knowledge."

"Your failure to obey is putting our invasion of Earth at risk," said Brainiac Prime. "Therefore, you are a threat to the mission. Therefore, you must be deleted!"

CHAPTER 4

BRAINIAC VS. BRAINIAC

WOOOOSH! Brainiac Prime flew at Supergirl. The rest of the robotic copies swooped down to attack as well.

From inside her brain, Brainiac fired Supergirl's heat vision. **ZAP!** It melted two of Brainiac Prime's robots.

"Quit using my powers!" said Supergirl.

"Stop arguing with me," Brainiac ordered Supergirl. "We will survive this attack only if you submit to my superior intellect."

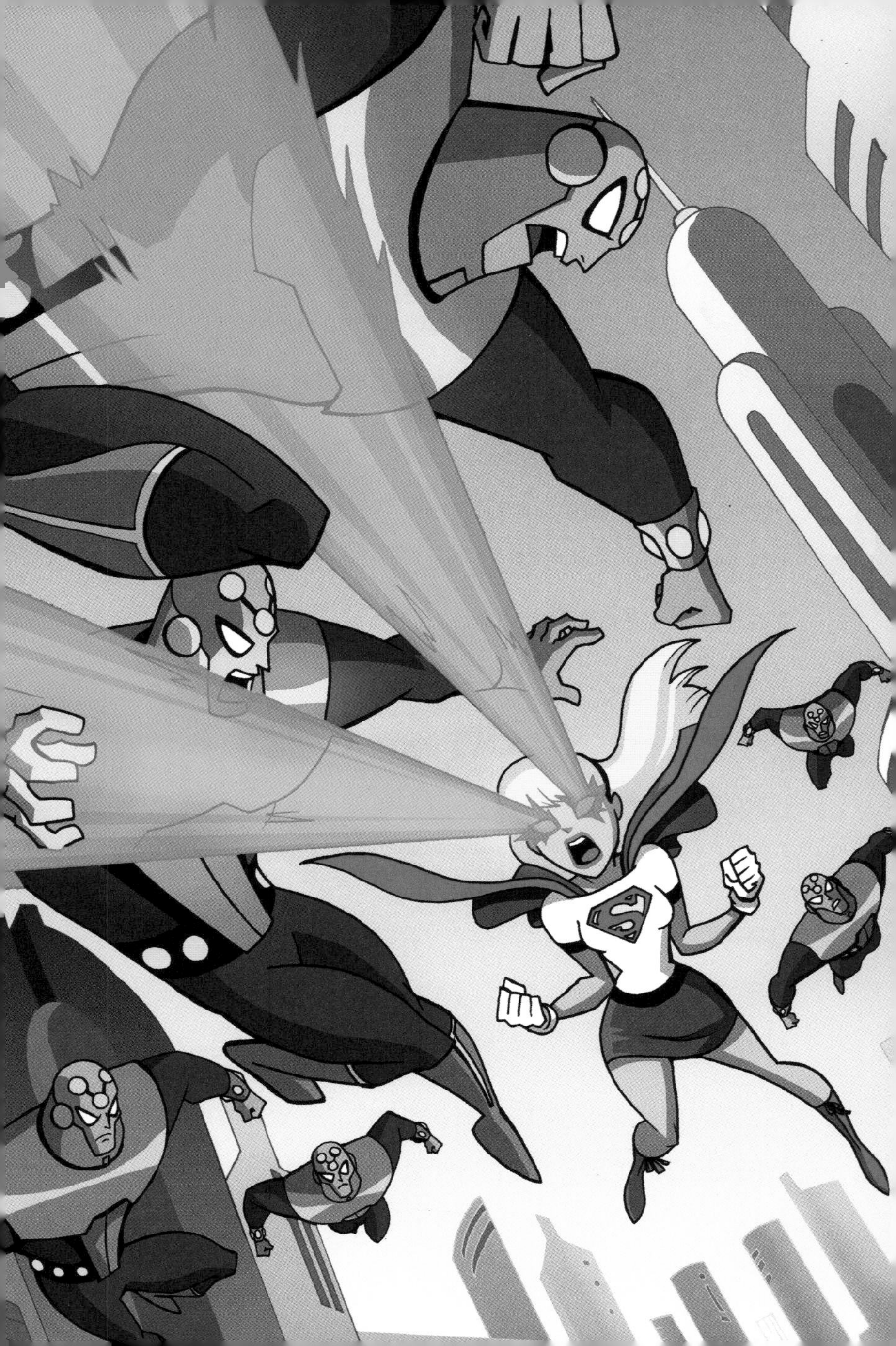

"Superior?" said Supergirl. "You can't even win an argument against yourself!"

Distracted, Braniac could not move Supergirl's muscles in time. **KA-POW!** Brainiac Prime slammed her to the ground.

"But I do know myself," Brainiac told Supergirl. "For example, I calculate that there is an 89.6% chance that Brainiac Prime will now telescope out his fists and attack you from both sides."

WHAM! BAM! Brainiac Prime attacked exactly as Brainiac predicted.

"Ow!" cried Supergirl. She was as strong and invulnerable as Superman, but she felt the impacts. "Okay, you've got a point," she admitted. "So what's your plan?"

"Observe," said Brainiac. "I will now implement Tactical Stratagem #7."

Brainiac commanded Supergirl's body to fly high into the air. **SWOOSH!** With Brainiac in control, Supergirl flew down at Brainiac Prime. **FWAZIIIIRP!** Brainiac directed Supergirl's heat vision to blast the ground beneath Brainiac Prime's feet.

"Stratagem #7," said Brainiac Prime, recognizing the attack. "A logical choice. But it will not work."

Brainiac Prime easily avoided Brainiac's attack. Then he swung a heavy metal fist at Supergirl. **BAM!** Brainiac Prime punched her, sending her spiraling backward. **BOOM!** She crashed through a building and landed hard in the street below.

"That was your big plan?" Supergirl shouted at Brainiac. "That was totally weak! He knows your moves as well as you know his."

"Of course," said Brainiac. "He and I are identical copies of the same program."

"Then if we're going to beat him," said Supergirl. "We have to do like Captain Joey says in 'Hob's Bay Hairspray' — 'When your ideas are totally stinking, come up with a surprising way of thinking!'"

"I am not familiar with that expression," replied Brainiac.

"Exactly!" said Supergirl. "But I am. You have to let me take control. You may know a ton of junk that I don't. But I know a thing or two that you don't. Which means Brainiac Prime won't see them coming."

WHIRRRRRR.

Brainiac's servos analyzed Supergirl's request. Then Brainiac said, "I concur. My calculations show that it is our best chance of survival."

Deep inside her brain, Brainiac moved away from the neurons that controlled Supergirl's body.

"Ungh!" Supergirl grunted. Her muscles and tendons came back under her own control. She flexed her fingers.

"Man, does it feel good to be in control of my own body again," she said, smirking.

WHOMP! WHOMP! WHOMP!

Brainiac Prime and several robot copies landed on the street in front of Supergirl. Brainiac Prime pointed at Supergirl. "Delete her," he ordered his robots.

As the robots flew at her, Supergirl quickly scanned the tall building next to her with her X-ray vision. Everyone in this part of the city had fled when Brainiac began his attack, so no one was inside the office tower now.

Supergirl turned back to face the robots. They zoomed closer and closer, but Supergirl just stood there.

"Hurry," ordered Brainiac. "Brainiac Prime's robots will be upon us shortly."

"Just relax," Supergirl said. "It's under control."

Just as the robot copies were about to reach her, Supergirl moved. In a blur of super-speed, she slammed into the empty skyscraper with her shoulder.

RUMMMMMBLE!! The building crashed down to the street like a wave. Tons and tons of cement and steel crushed all the robots into tiny metal bits. Now, the only ones standing in the street were Supergirl and Brainiac Prime.

"Impressive," said Brainiac Prime.

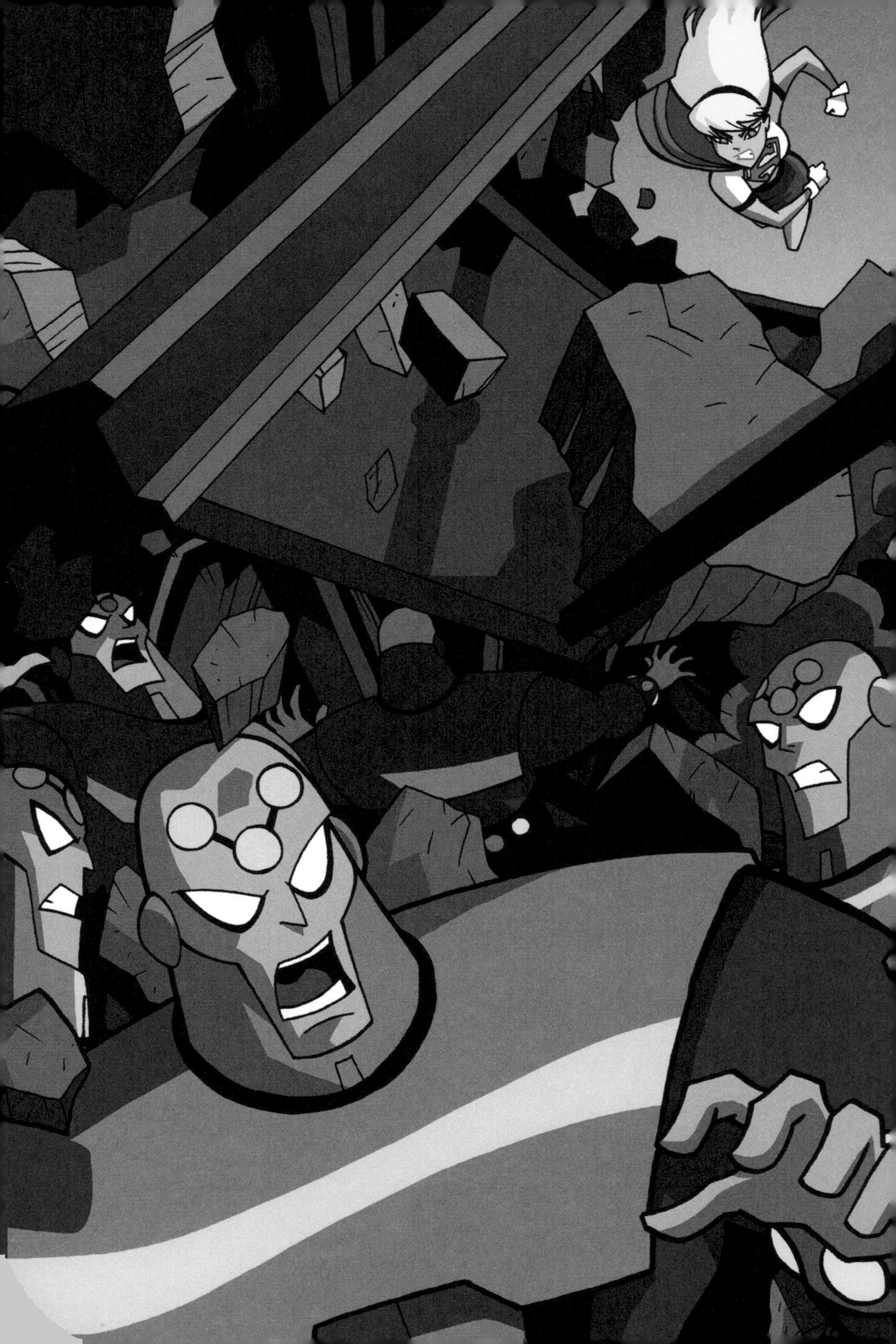

"I concur," said Brainiac.

"I see that you are a much more imposing foe when Brainiac is not guiding you," Brainiac Prime told Supergirl. "I will not underestimate you again."

SHLOOP! Brainiac Prime's chest opened. A dozen thick metal cables slithered out. **FWAAP! FWAAP!** They coiled around her and squeezed.

"Okay, Brainiac," whispered Supergirl. "What do we do now?"

"I thought you were in charge of fighting this battle," replied Brainiac.

"That's what Brainiac Prime thinks too," whispered Supergirl. "Whatever you do right now, he won't it see coming!"

"The metal coils that are squeezing you are conductors of heat," said Brainiac.

"I would blast them with your heat vision," Brainiac suggested. "The heat will travel through them to the circuitry inside his body, making his systems overload."

"Done!" said Supergirl. **ZAP!** She hit the metal coils with her heat vision. The heat raced along the coils and into Brainiac Prime's body. **FOOOM!** The circuits connected to the coils burst into flames.

"GRAAARH!" cried Brainiac Prime. Suddenly, his eyes went blank, and he fell over and hit the street with a **CLUNK!**

"Sweet!" cried Supergirl. "We did it!"

"Indeed," replied Brainiac from inside her brain. "And now your usefulness to me has ended."

"ARRGH!" cried Supergirl, her body suddenly consumed by pain.

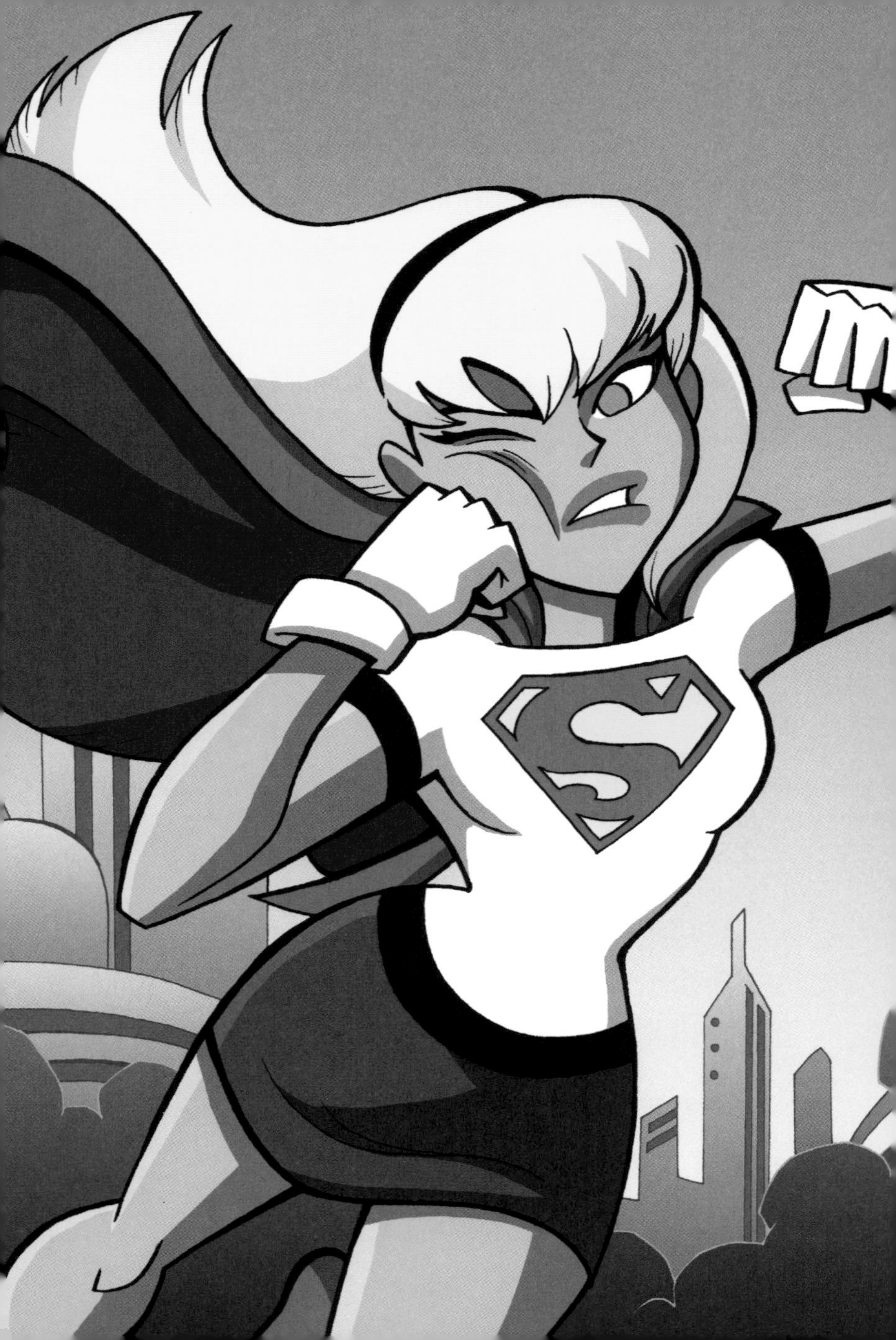

#

CHAPTER 5

Brainiac flew between the neurons that controlled Supergirl's right arm. **BAM!** **BAM!** Brainiac made Supergirl punch herself with her own fist again and again.

"Oh, come on!" cried Supergirl. "What are you, a third-grade bully?"

"No," replied Brainiac. "I am a twelfth-level intellect. I am also in complete control of your muscles. You cannot stop me."

Brainiac flew over to another set of neurons in Supergirl's brain. **ZAAAAP!** He made her fire out a blast of heat vision.

WHA-BOOOM! The blast hit an empty taxi. The car exploded into flames.

"Surrender your knowledge of Argo City," ordered Brainiac. "Or I will use your powers to destroy Metropolis."

"No!" pleaded Supergirl. She slumped her shoulders. "Fine, you win. You can have my memories of Argo City. All of them."

"I would imagine that you have only a few," said Brainiac, "since your head seems to be filled with trivial Earth memories. Tell me where your memories of Argo City are."

ZAP! A neuron fired an electrical burst. It was a memory of Argo City! Brainiac smiled a microscopic smile as he flew toward it. "Finally," he said. "I will now take what few valuable memories you have left . . . and then delete you."

"Do what you want with me," said Supergirl. "Just leave Metropolis alone."

Brainiac positioned himself between the neurons. "I make no such promises," he said. "Give me all your memories of Argo City! Now!"

"You asked for it!" said Supergirl.

She flooded her mind with memories of Argo City. Supergirl had thousands of them. And each memory was an electrical blast fired by a neuron. So many memories caused hundreds of thousands of neurons to fire their lightning bolts of electricity — all at once.

It was a literal brainstorm. And Brainiac was caught in the middle of it!

"ARGGG!" cried Brainiac, bombarded by blasts. "I was not expecting so many!"

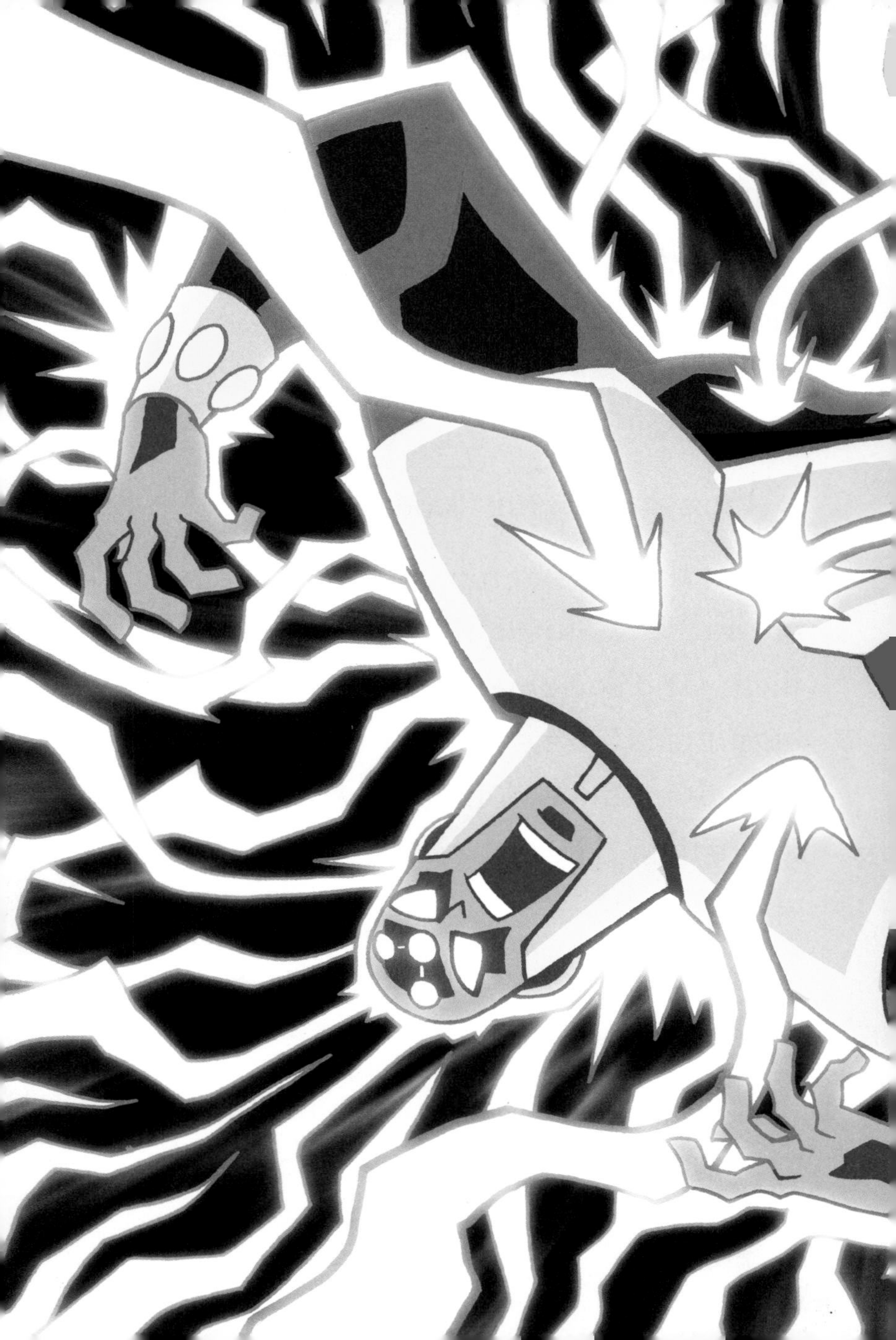

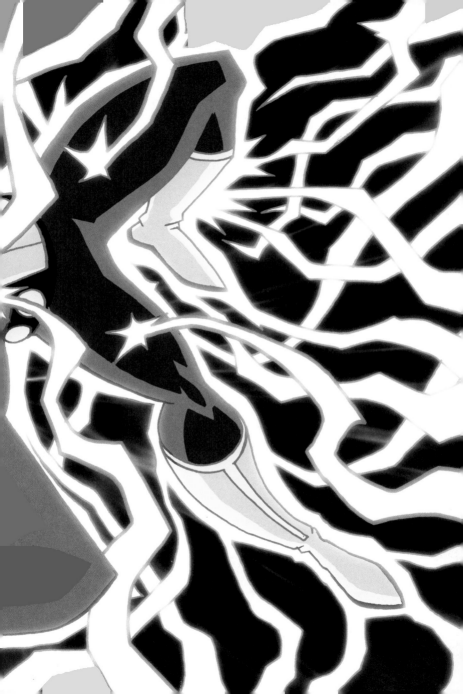

"You thought I had forgotten about Argo City?" shouted Supergirl. "It was my home! I haven't forgotten anything."

Supergirl blasted him with her memories. **FWAZAP! FWAZAP! FWAZAP!** They hit him from all sides.

"I may spend a lot of time thinking about Captain Joey and that other stuff," said Supergirl, "but that's because Earth is my home now. Just because I think about malls and Earth boys doesn't mean I've forgotten where I'm from. Or who I am."

"YAURRRGH!" wailed Brainiac, unprepared for the massive electrical attack. His microscopic body could not absorb this many blasts at once.

"Maybe you'd have known that if you'd ever been inside a teenager's head before!" said Supergirl.

FWAZAPP! Electricity surged through Brainiac. **TZZZT!** Circuits fried as his systems overloaded. One by one, they began to shut down. The electrical mind-storm was only getting more intense as Supergirl remembered more and more.

Brainiac had no choice but to retreat from Supergirl's body. **WHHOOOSH!** He flew out of Supergirl's ear. She could tell immediately that he was gone. "And stay out!" she shouted.

The gentle breeze that floated through Metropolis lifted Brainiac up and sent him swirling into the sky. **WOOOOOSH!** He spun wildly through the air, unable to stop.

As he drifted away to wherever the wind was taking him, all Brainiac could do to make himself feel better was vow never to experience a teenager's mind again.

SUPER HEROES VS.

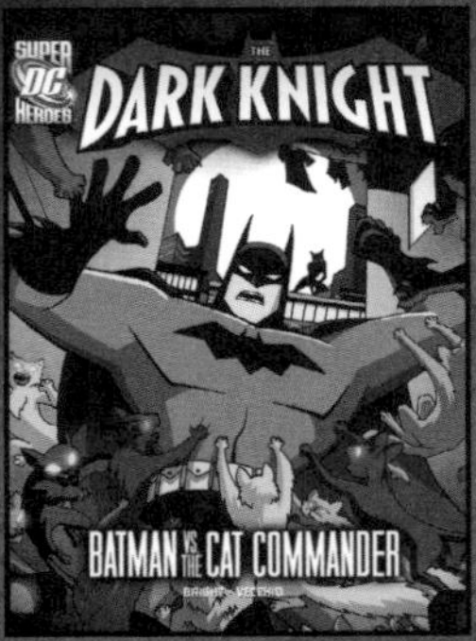
SUPER DC HEROES
THE DARK KNIGHT
BATMAN VS THE CAT COMMANDER

BATMAN VS. THE CAT COMMANDER

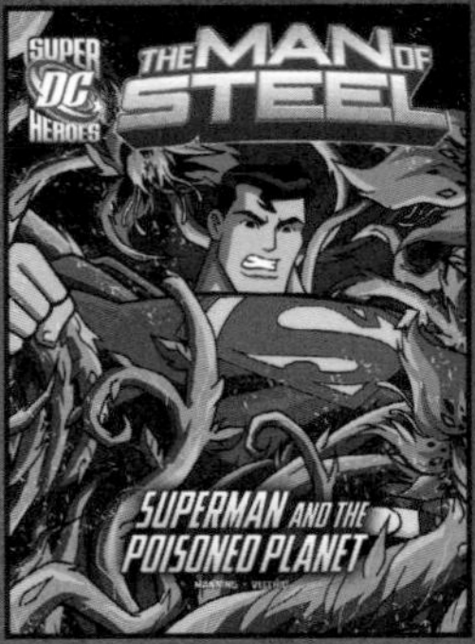
SUPER DC HEROES
THE MAN OF STEEL
SUPERMAN AND THE POISONED PLANET

SUPERMAN AND THE POISONED PLANET

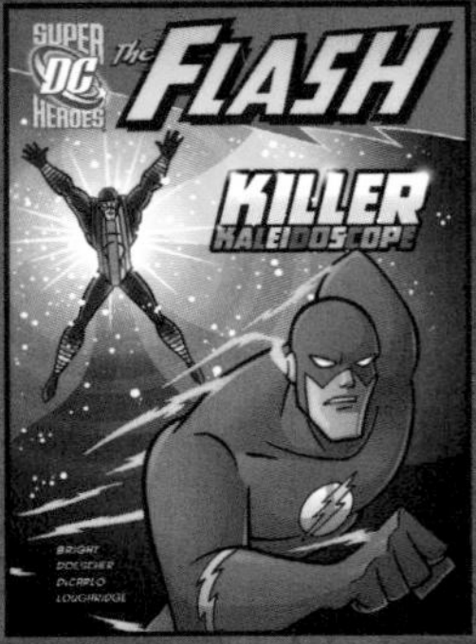
SUPER DC HEROES
The FLASH
KILLER KALEIDOSCOPE

THE FLASH: KILLER KALEIDOSCOPE

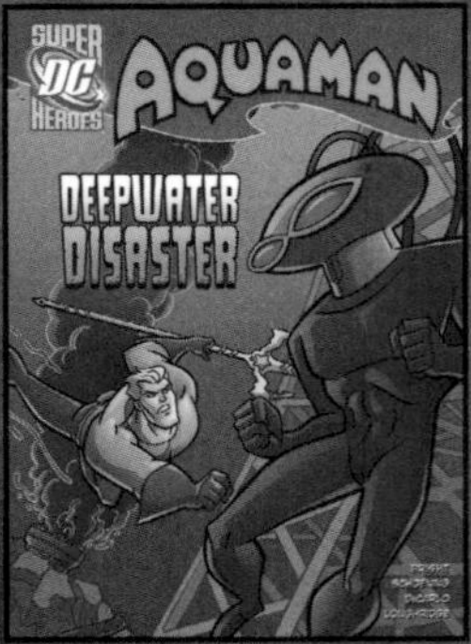
SUPER DC HEROES
AQUAMAN
DEEPWATER DISASTER

AQUAMAN: DEEPWATER DISASTER

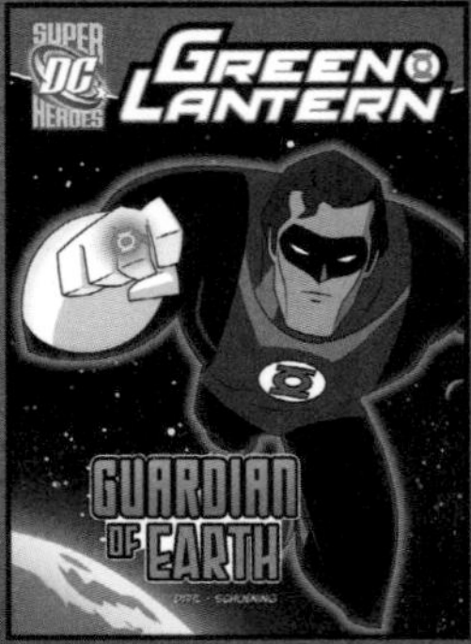
SUPER DC HEROES
GREEN LANTERN
GUARDIAN OF EARTH

GREEN LANTERN: GUARDIAN OF EARTH

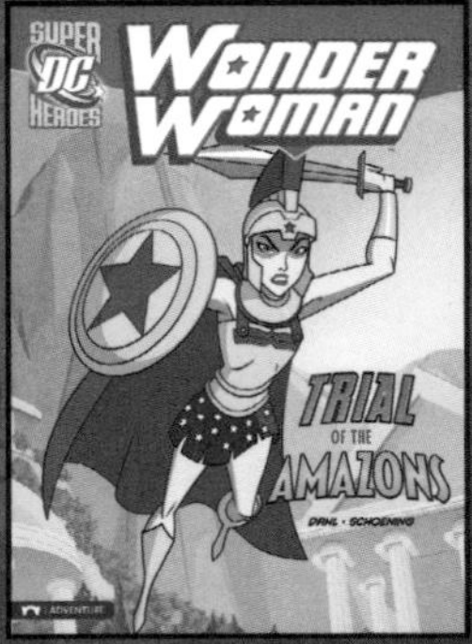
SUPER DC HEROES
WONDER WOMAN
TRIAL OF THE AMAZONS

WONDER WOMAN: TRIAL OF THE AMAZONS

WHICH SIDE...

SUPER-VILLAINS

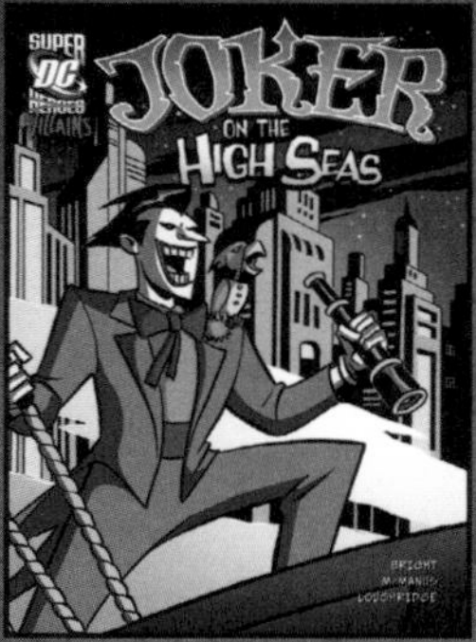
SUPER DC HEROES VILLAINS
JOKER
ON THE
HIGH SEAS

JOKER ON THE HIGH SEAS

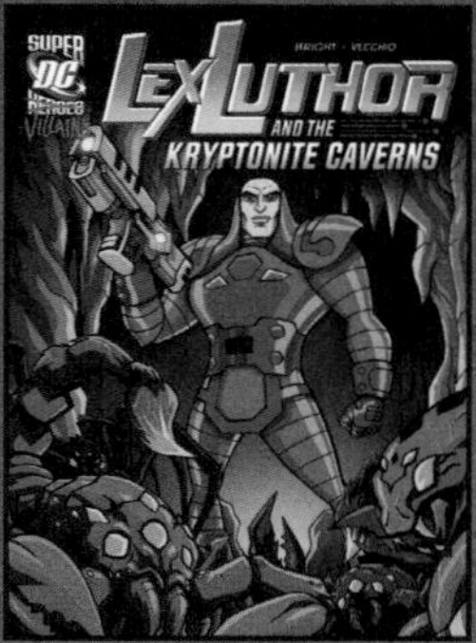
SUPER DC HEROES VILLAINS
LEX LUTHOR
AND THE
KRYPTONITE CAVERNS

LEX LUTHOR AND THE KRYPTONITE CAVERNS

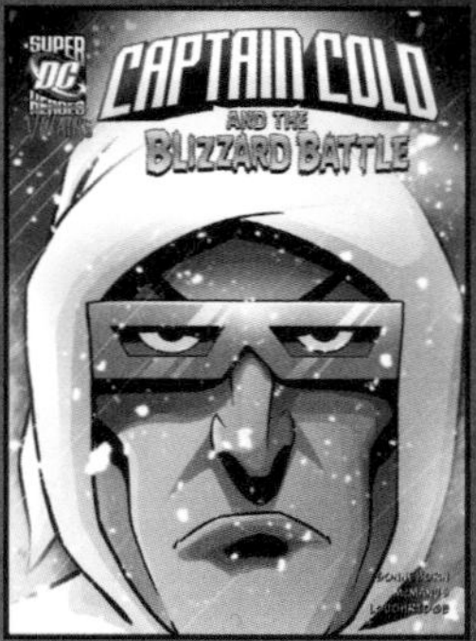
SUPER DC HEROES VILLAINS
CAPTAIN COLD
AND THE
BLIZZARD BATTLE

CAPTAIN COLD AND THE BLIZZARD BATTLE

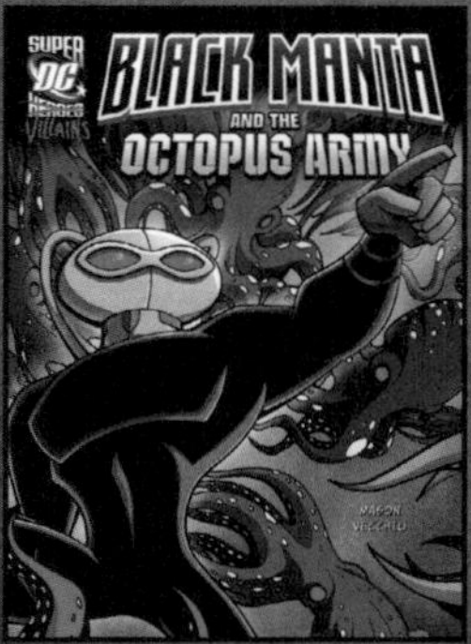
SUPER DC HEROES VILLAINS
BLACK MANTA
AND THE
OCTOPUS ARMY

BLACK MANTA AND THE OCTOPUS ARMY

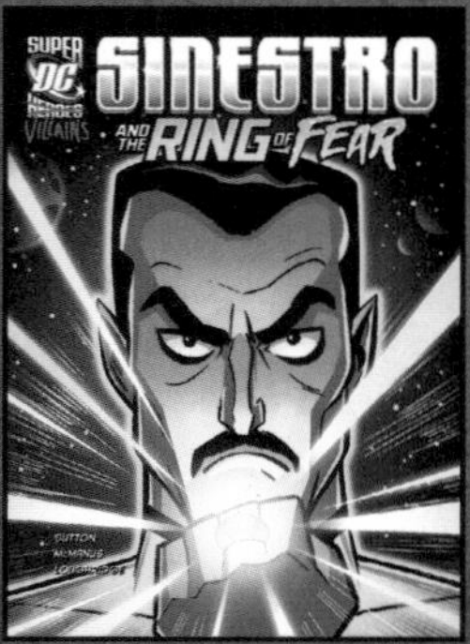
SUPER DC HEROES VILLAINS
SINESTRO
AND THE RING OF FEAR

SINESTRO AND THE RING OF FEAR

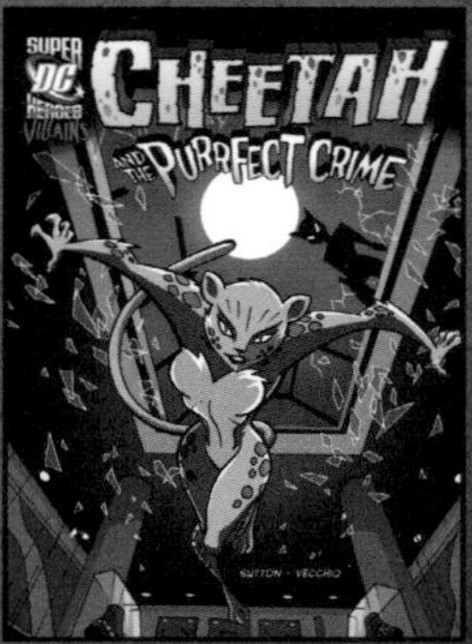
SUPER DC HEROES VILLAINS
CHEETAH
AND THE PURRFECT CRIME
SUTTON · VECCHIO

CHEETAH AND THE PURRFECT CRIME

WILL YOU CHOOSE?

IF YOU WERE SUPERGIRL

Supergirl uses her heat vision to melt one of Brainiac's drones. If you were capable of using heat vision, what would you use the superpower to do?

Supergirl possesses super-strength. In what ways would being incredibly strong come in handy? Are there any drawbacks to having super-strength?

IF YOU WERE BRAINIAC

Brainiac built several copies of himself. If you could make copies of yourself, what would you do with your identical drones?

Brainiac uses his telescopic fists to attack Supergirl. Of all the powers and abilities that Brainiac and Supergirl use in this book, which one would you want the most? Why?

AUTHOR BIO

Scott Sonneborn has written 20 books, one circus (for Ringling Bros. Barnum & Bailey), and a bunch of TV shows. He's been nominated for one Emmy and spent three very cool years working at DC Comics. He lives in Los Angeles with his wife and their two sons.

SUPER HERO GLOSSARY

heat vision (HEET VIZH-uhn)—Supergirl can emit powerful rays from her eyes

invulnerable (in-VUHL-ner-uh-buhl)—unable to be harmed or damaged, like Supergirl and Superman

Krypton (KRIP-tahn)—Supergirl's home planet

Kryptonian (krip-TOHN-ee-uhn)—from Krypton

S-shield (ESS-sheeld)—the "s" that is on Supergirl's costume

X-ray vision (EKS-ray VIZH-uhn)—Supergirl can see through solid objects (except for lead)

ILLUSTRATOR BIO

Luciano Vecchio was born in 1982 and currently lives in Buenos Aires, Argentina. With experience in illustration, animation, and comics, his works have been published in the US, Spain, UK, France, and Argentina. His credits include Ben 10 (DC Comics), Cruel Thing (Norma), Unseen Tribe (Zuda Comics), and Sentinels (Drumfish Productions).

SUPER-VILLAIN GLOSSARY

drones (DROHNZ)—slaves, like Brainiac's drones

fierce (FEERSS)—violent or intense, like Brainiac's invasion of Metropolis

sinister (SIN-uh-ster)—seeming evil and threatening, like Brainiac's glowing red eyes

tentacles (TEN-tuh-kuhls)—long, flexible limbs, like Brainiac's telescopic arms

threat (THRET)—something regarded as likely to be dangerous, like evil flying robots

twelfth-level intellect—a high level of intelligence. Brainiac is a twelfth level intellect.

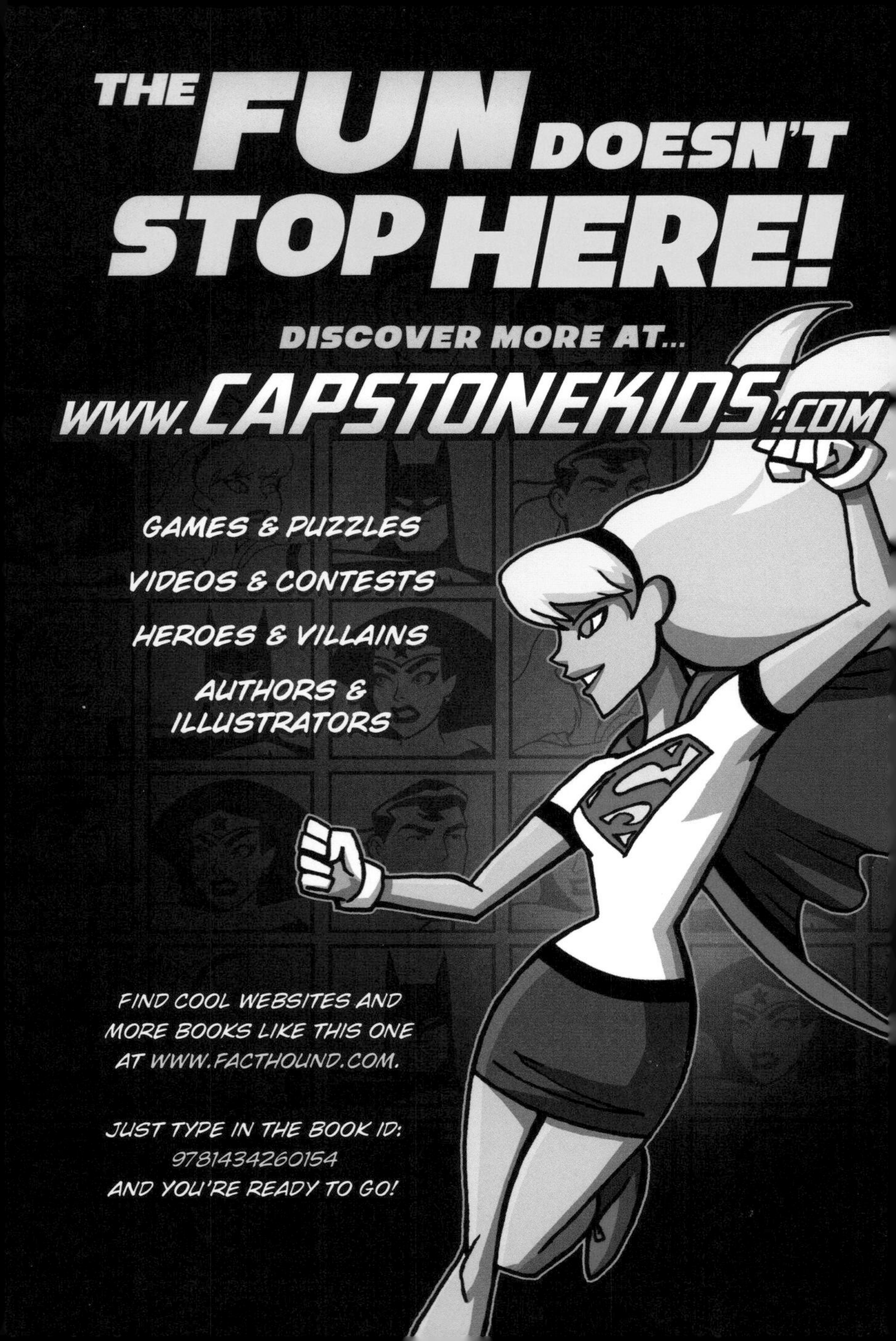
THE FUN DOESN'T STOP HERE!
DISCOVER MORE AT...
WWW.CAPSTONEKIDS.COM
GAMES & PUZZLES
VIDEOS & CONTESTS
HEROES & VILLAINS
AUTHORS & ILLUSTRATORS
FIND COOL WEBSITES AND MORE BOOKS LIKE THIS ONE AT WWW.FACTHOUND.COM.
JUST TYPE IN THE BOOK ID: 9781434260154 AND YOU'RE READY TO GO!

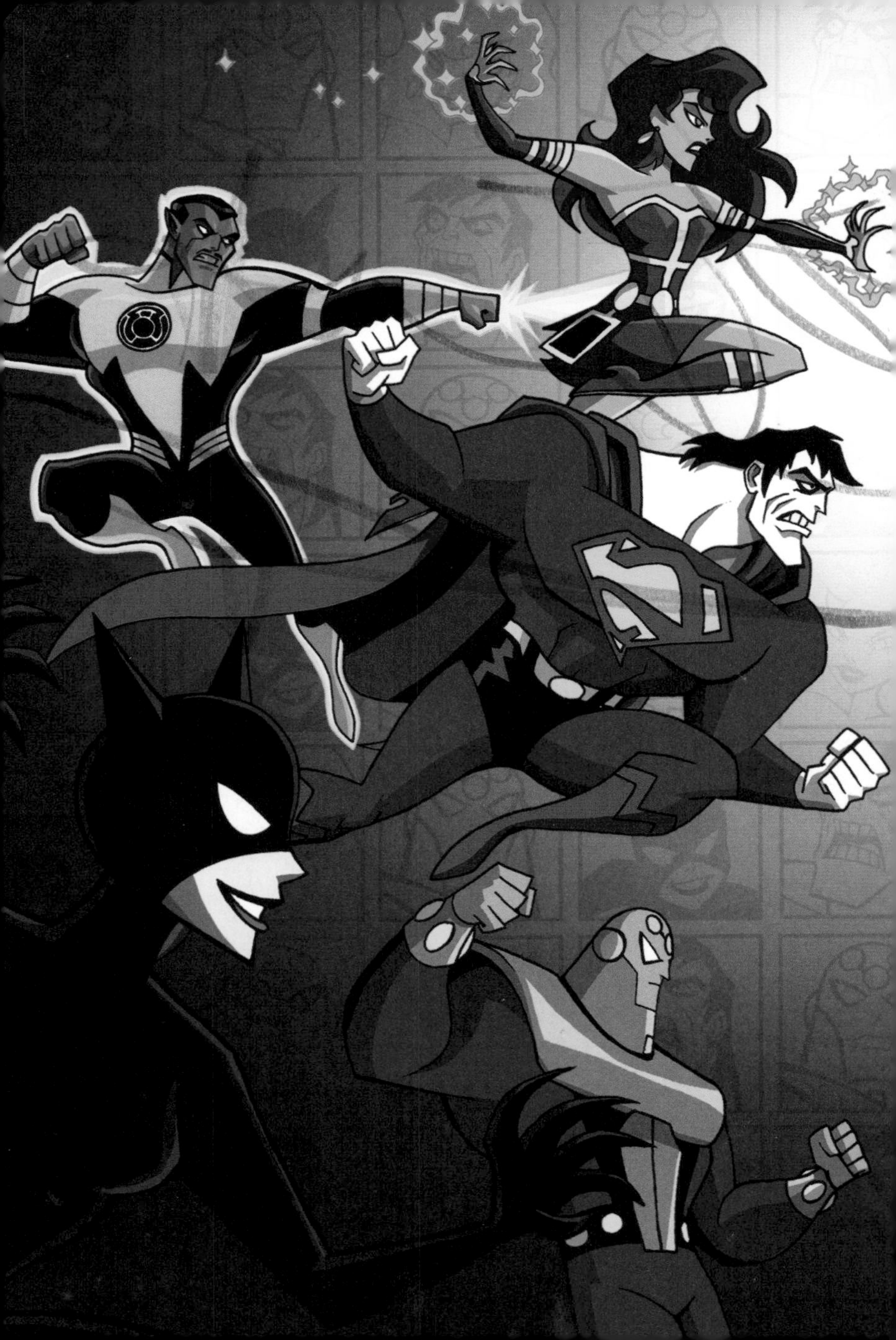

BLOOMFIELD TOWNSHIP PUBLIC LIBRARY

3 1160 00372 1359

W9-CNA-344

BLOOMFIELD TOWNSHIP PUBLIC LIBRARY
1099 Lone Pine Road
Bloomfield Hills, Michigan 48302-2410

waking upside down

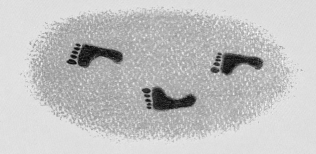

waking

by PHILIP HECKMAN

illustrated by DWIGHT BEEN

upside down

Atheneum Books for Young Readers

BLOOMFIELD TOWNSHIP PUBLIC LIBRARY
1099 Lone Pine Road
Bloomfield Hills, Michigan 48302-2410

Atheneum Books for Young Readers
An imprint of Simon & Schuster Children's Publishing Division
1230 Avenue of the Americas
New York, New York 10020

Text copyright © 1996 by Philip Heckman
Illustrations copyright © 1996 by Dwight Been
All rights reserved including the right of reproduction in whole or in part in any form.

Designed by Angela Carlino
The text of this book is set in Matrix.
The illustrations were rendered in watercolors and colored pencils.

Manufactured in the United States of America
First edition
10 9 8 7 6 5 4 3 2 1

Library of Congress Cataloging-in-Publication Data
Heckman, Philip.
Waking upside down / by Philip Heckman ; illustrated by Dwight Been.
p.   cm.
Summary: Morton is angry at having to trade bedrooms with his twin sisters, but the first time he sleeps in their old room, he wakes up in the middle of the night with a mysterious new talent that cheers him up.
ISBN 0-689-31930-4
[1. Brothers and sisters—Fiction.   2. Bedrooms—Fiction.   3. Family life—Fiction.]
I. Been, Dwight, ill. II. Title.
PZ7.H3553Wak   1996
[E]—dc20
95-7746

To Mom and Dad, for giving me the run of the house
while they were sleeping

—P. H.

To my mother and father with love

—D.B.

NOV 1 4 1996 B & TAYLOR

Morton went to bed angry. Earlier that day his parents had told him his twin sisters needed more space, so Morton had to give up his big bedroom for their tiny one.

Now Morton looked around at the little girls' bunny rabbit wallpaper and the night sky they'd pasted on the ceiling. This was not fair. Nobody could sleep in such a stupid room, he thought.

But finally he did.

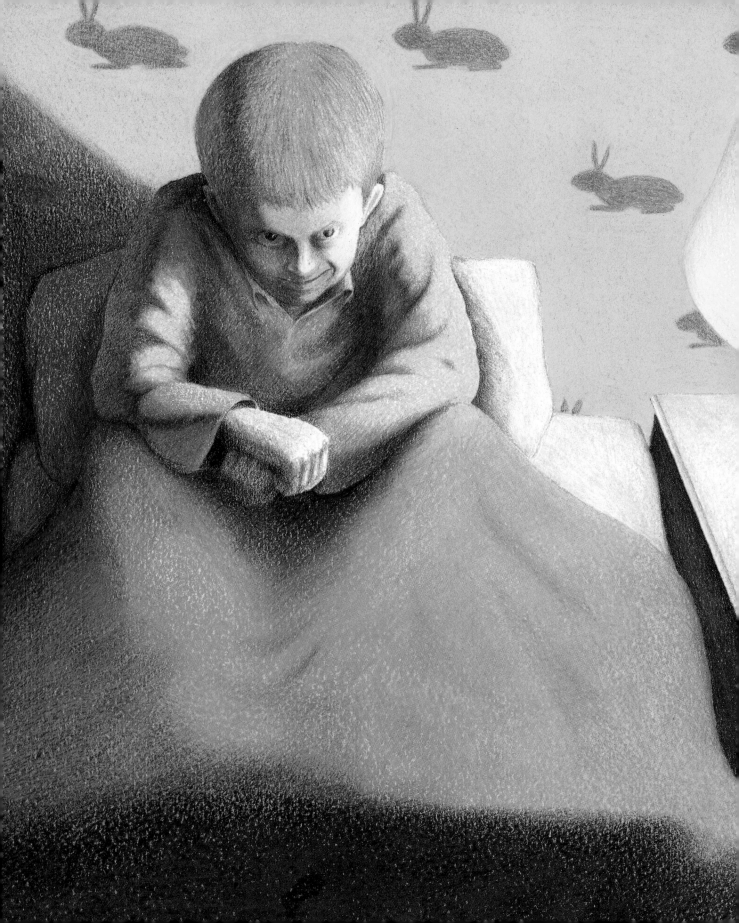

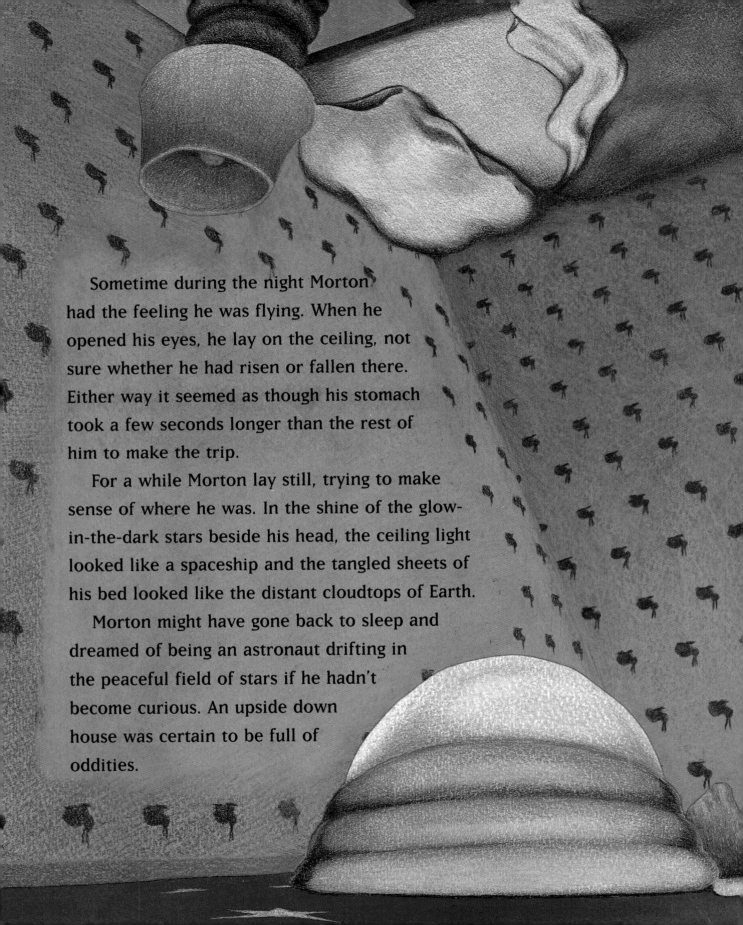

Sometime during the night Morton had the feeling he was flying. When he opened his eyes, he lay on the ceiling, not sure whether he had risen or fallen there. Either way it seemed as though his stomach took a few seconds longer than the rest of him to make the trip.

For a while Morton lay still, trying to make sense of where he was. In the shine of the glow-in-the-dark stars beside his head, the ceiling light looked like a spaceship and the tangled sheets of his bed looked like the distant cloudtops of Earth.

Morton might have gone back to sleep and dreamed of being an astronaut drifting in the peaceful field of stars if he hadn't become curious. An upside down house was certain to be full of oddities.

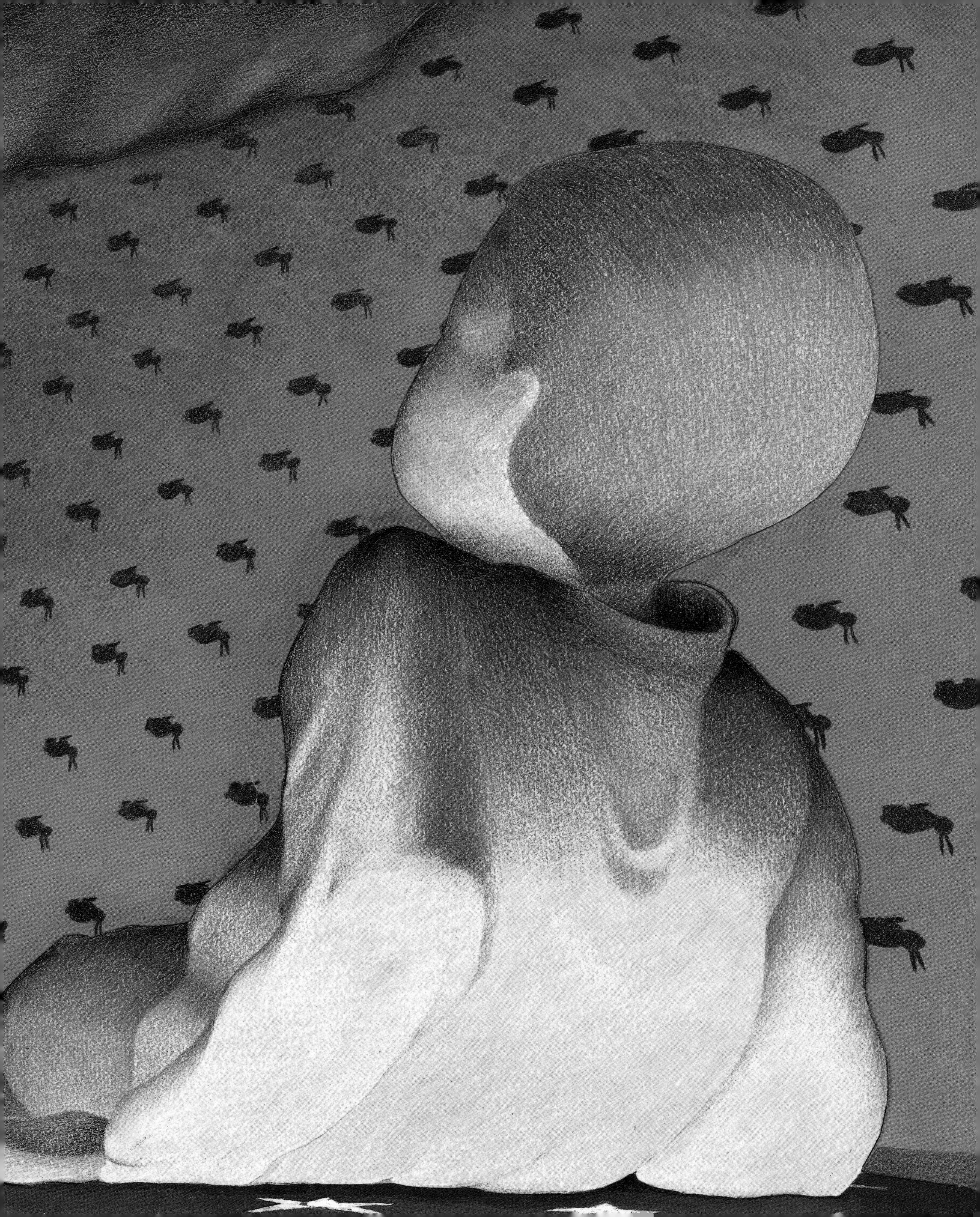

Morton got to his feet and carefully stepped through his bedroom doorway. All around him once familiar sights now seemed impossible.

How did water stay in the toilet bowl? he wondered. And how did dust settle on *this* edge of the door? Gravity, of course. Morton knew all about gravity, but until then it had seemed dull and ordinary. Viewed upside down, gravity was a suprise that made him dance with delight.

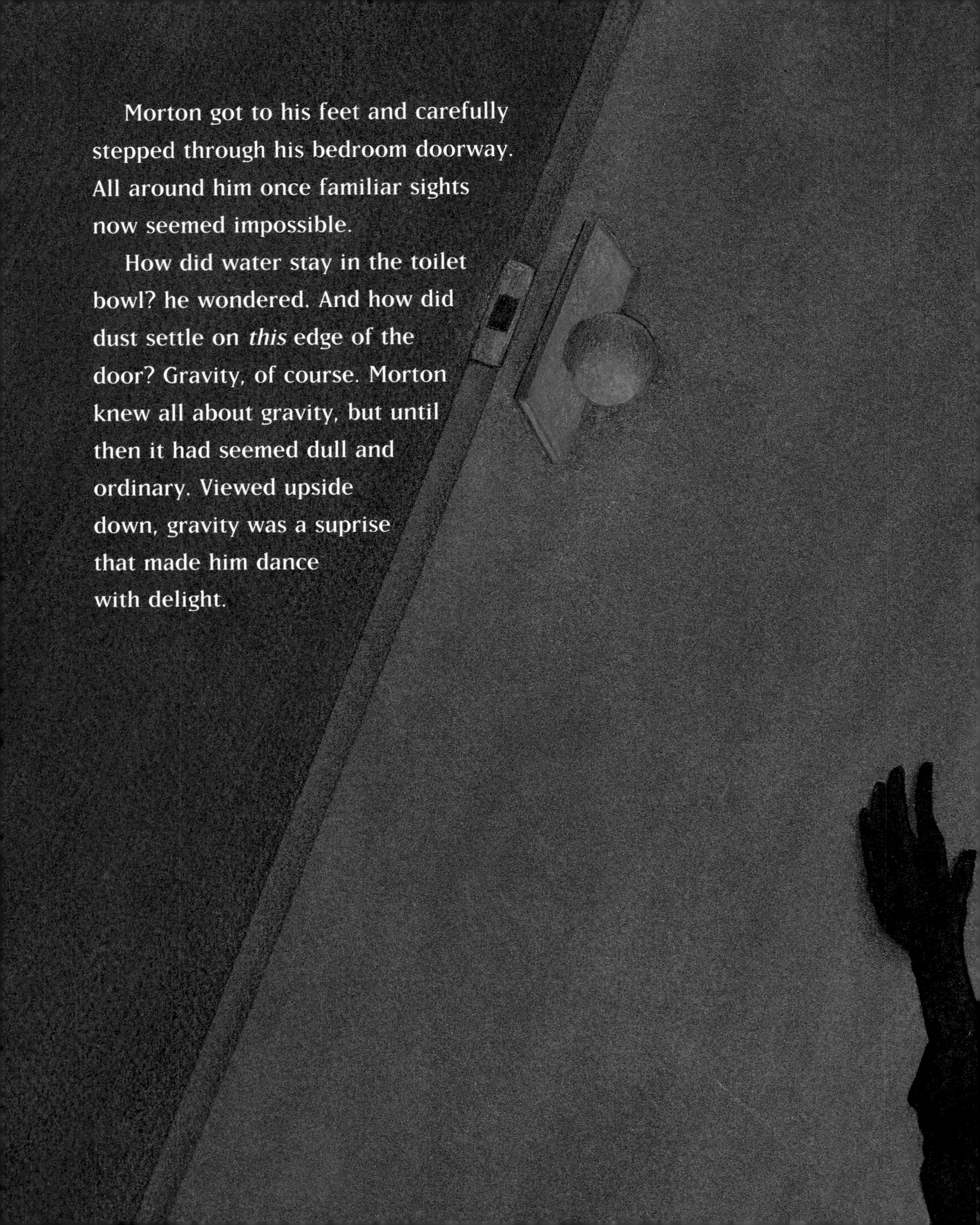

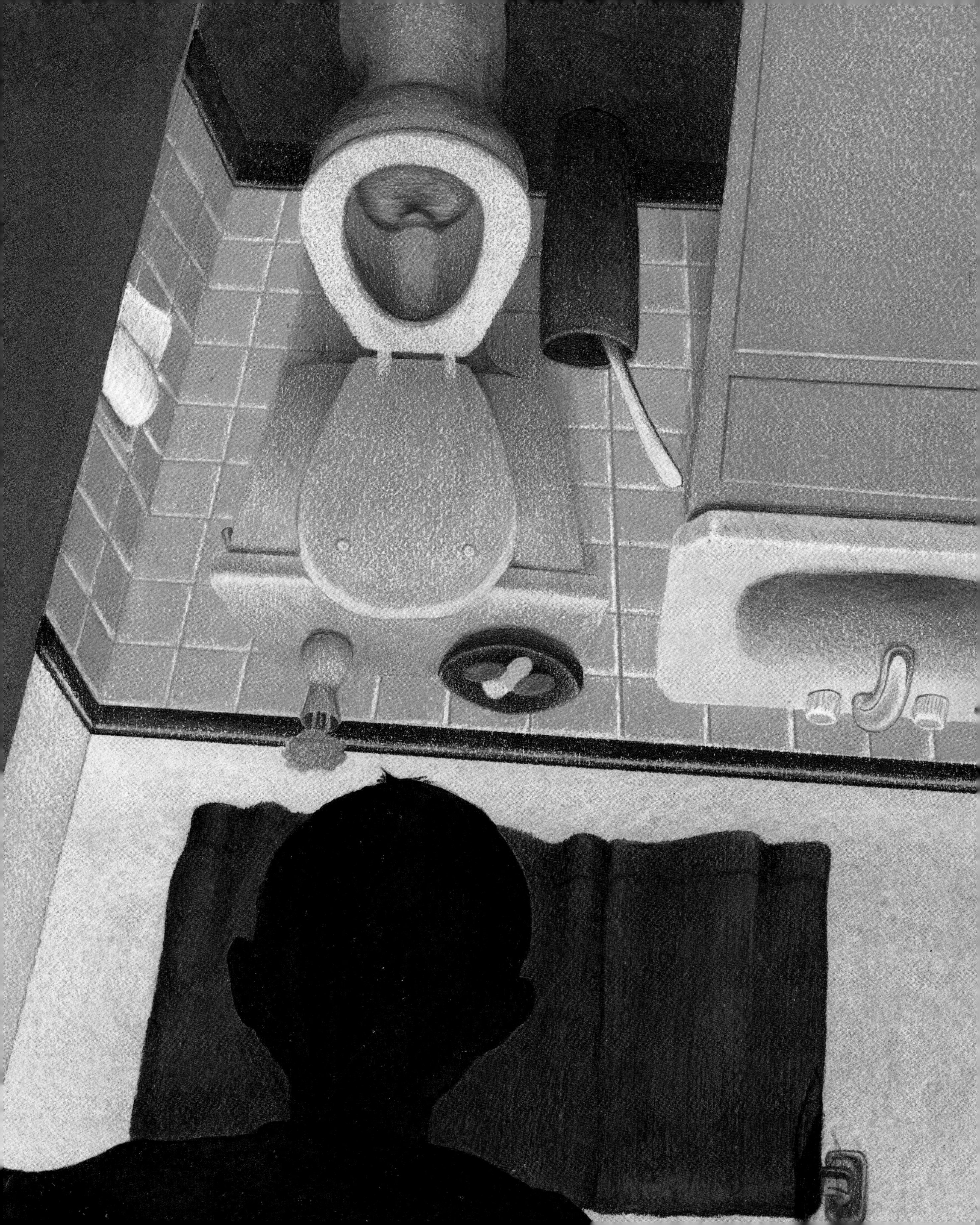

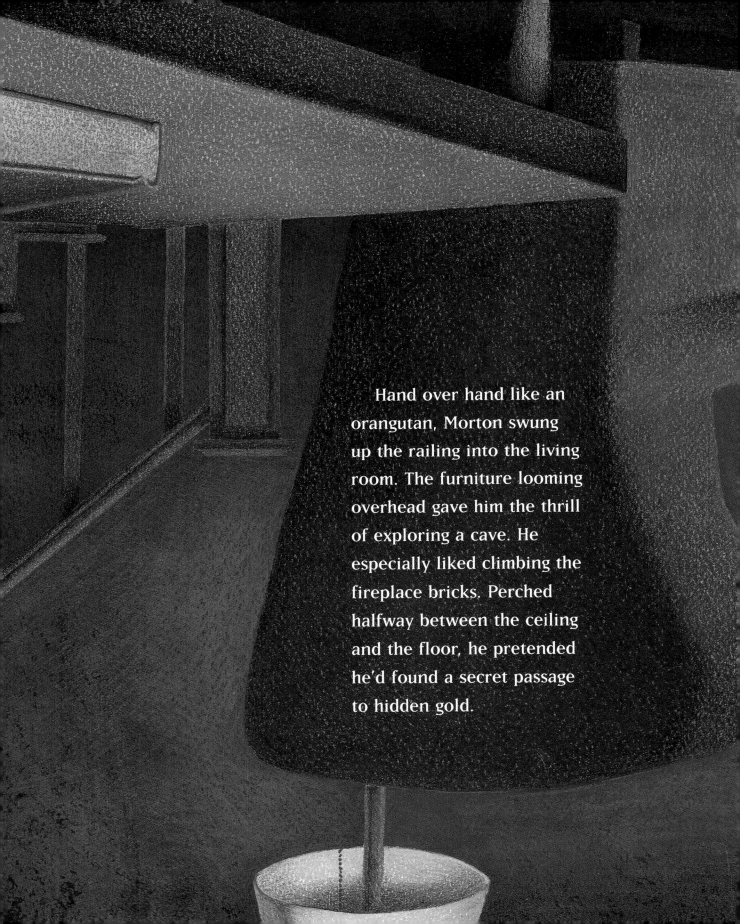

Hand over hand like an orangutan, Morton swung up the railing into the living room. The furniture looming overhead gave him the thrill of exploring a cave. He especially liked climbing the fireplace bricks. Perched halfway between the ceiling and the floor, he pretended he'd found a secret passage to hidden gold.

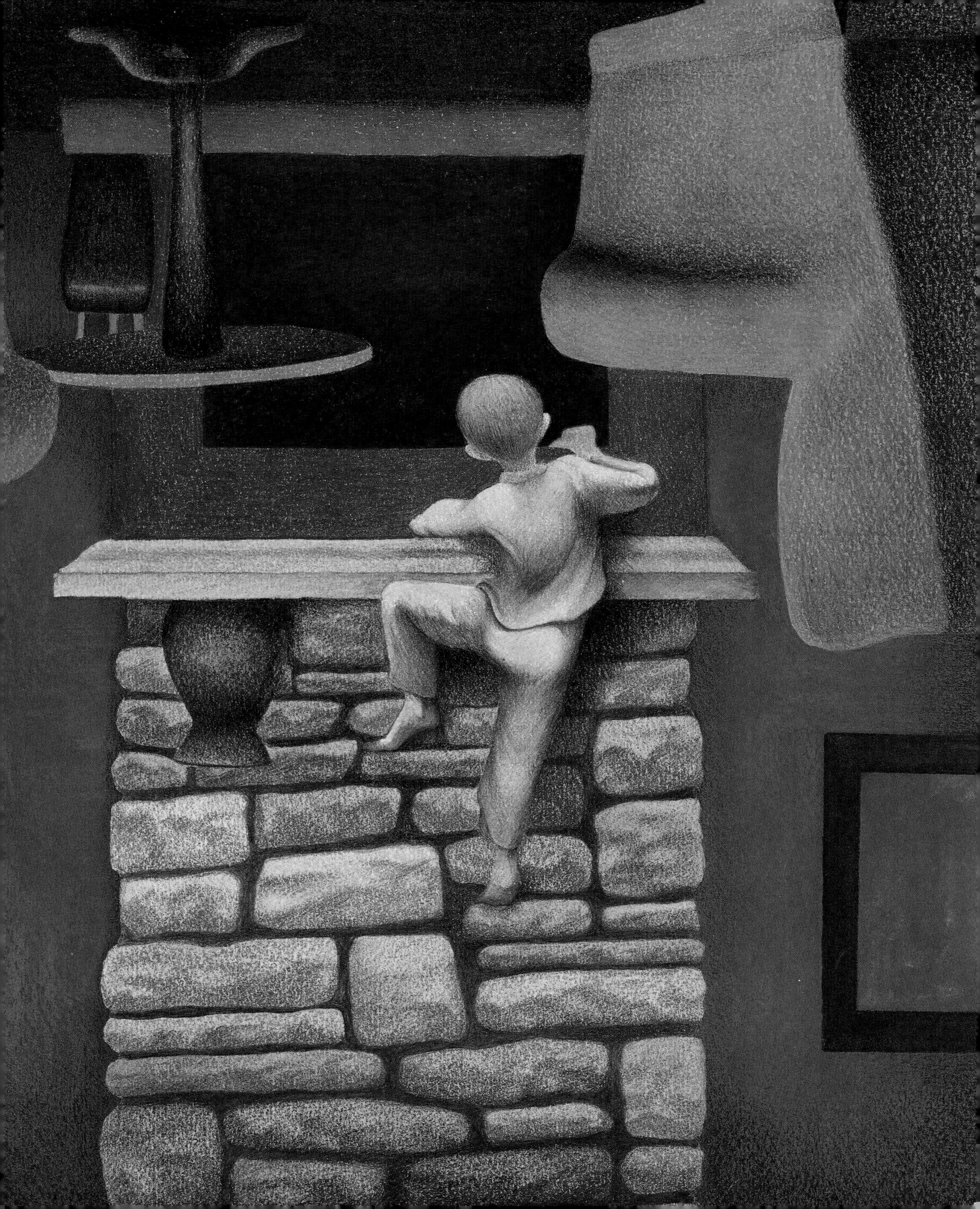

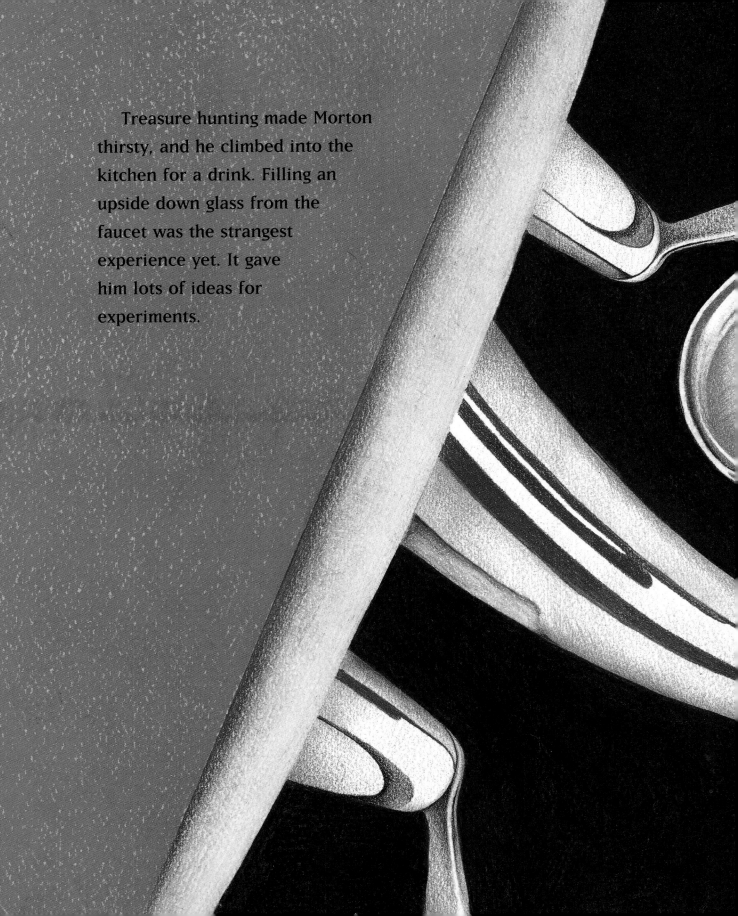

Treasure hunting made Morton thirsty, and he climbed into the kitchen for a drink. Filling an upside down glass from the faucet was the strangest experience yet. It gave him lots of ideas for experiments.

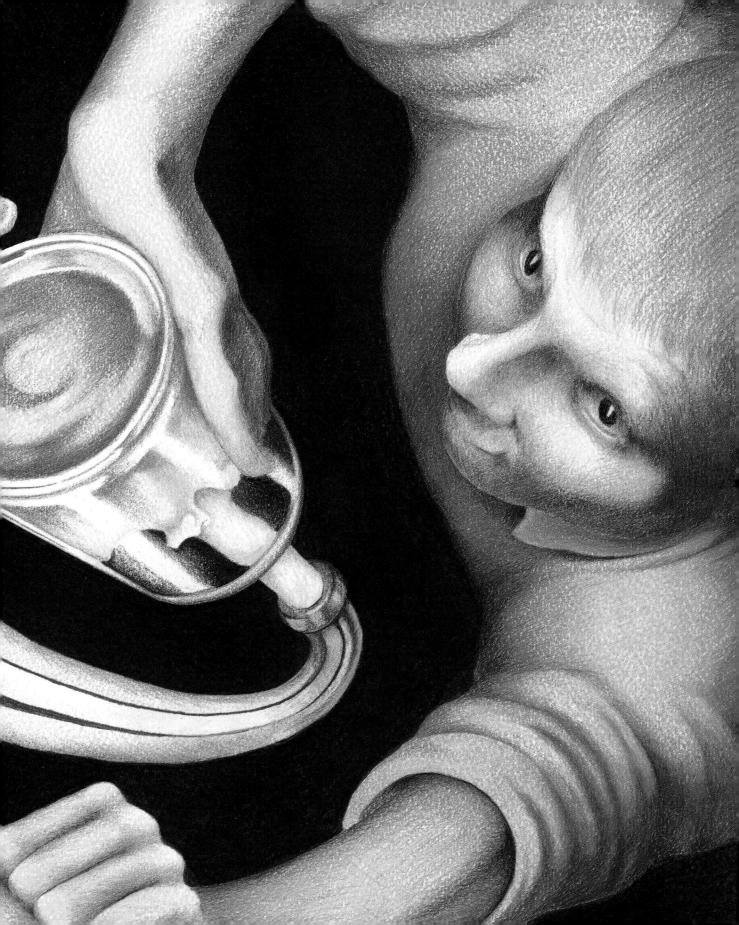

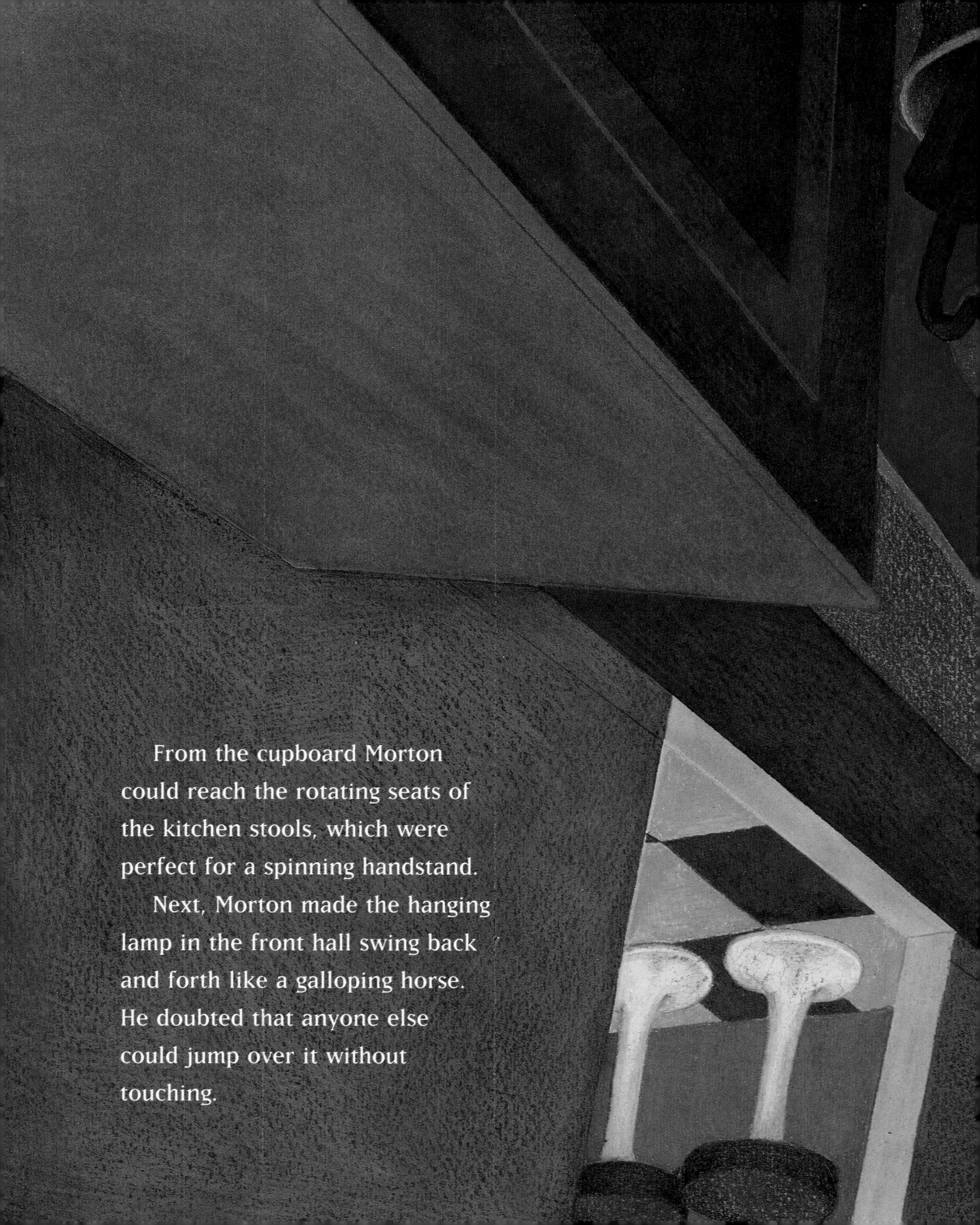

From the cupboard Morton could reach the rotating seats of the kitchen stools, which were perfect for a spinning handstand.

Next, Morton made the hanging lamp in the front hall swing back and forth like a galloping horse. He doubted that anyone else could jump over it without touching.

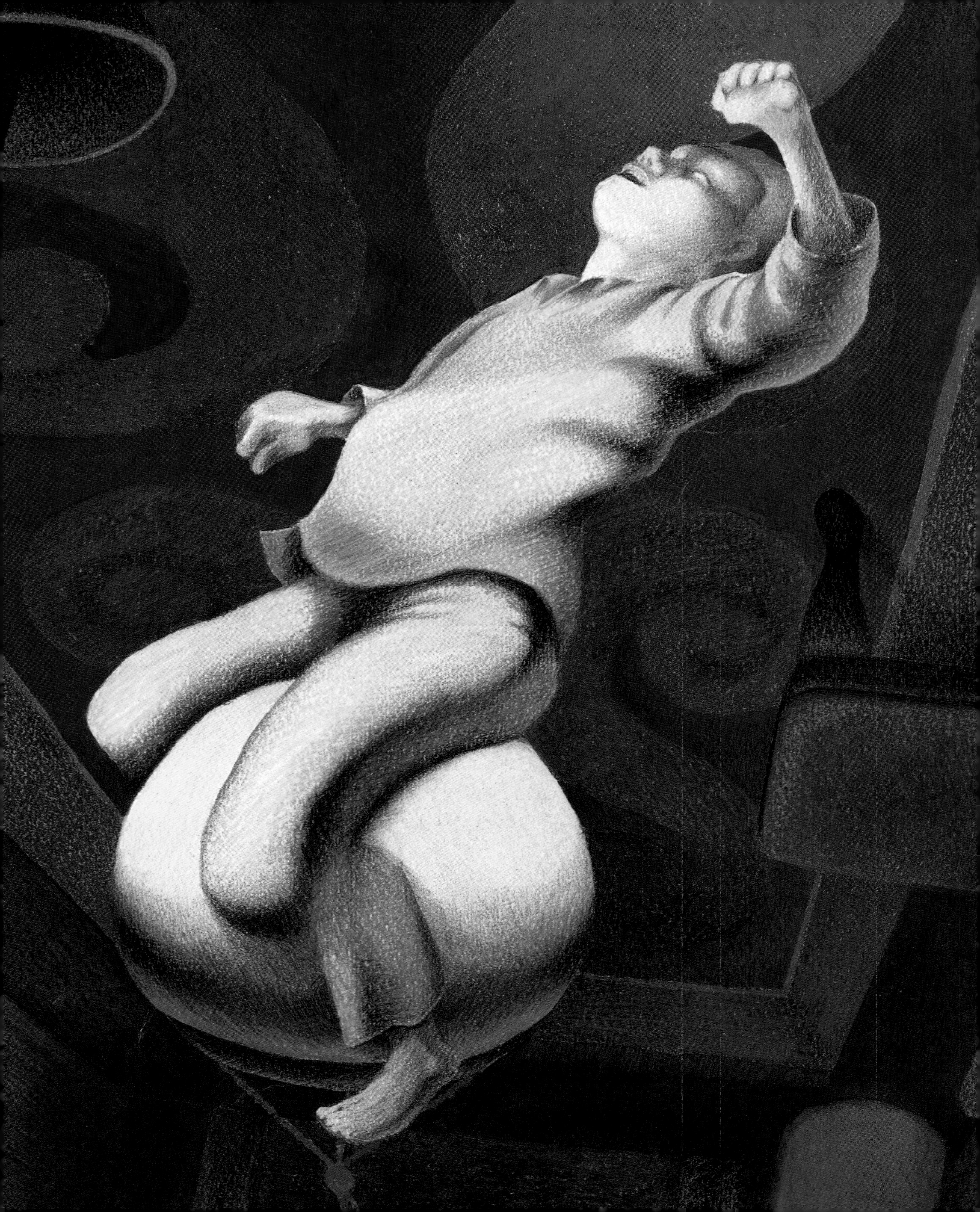

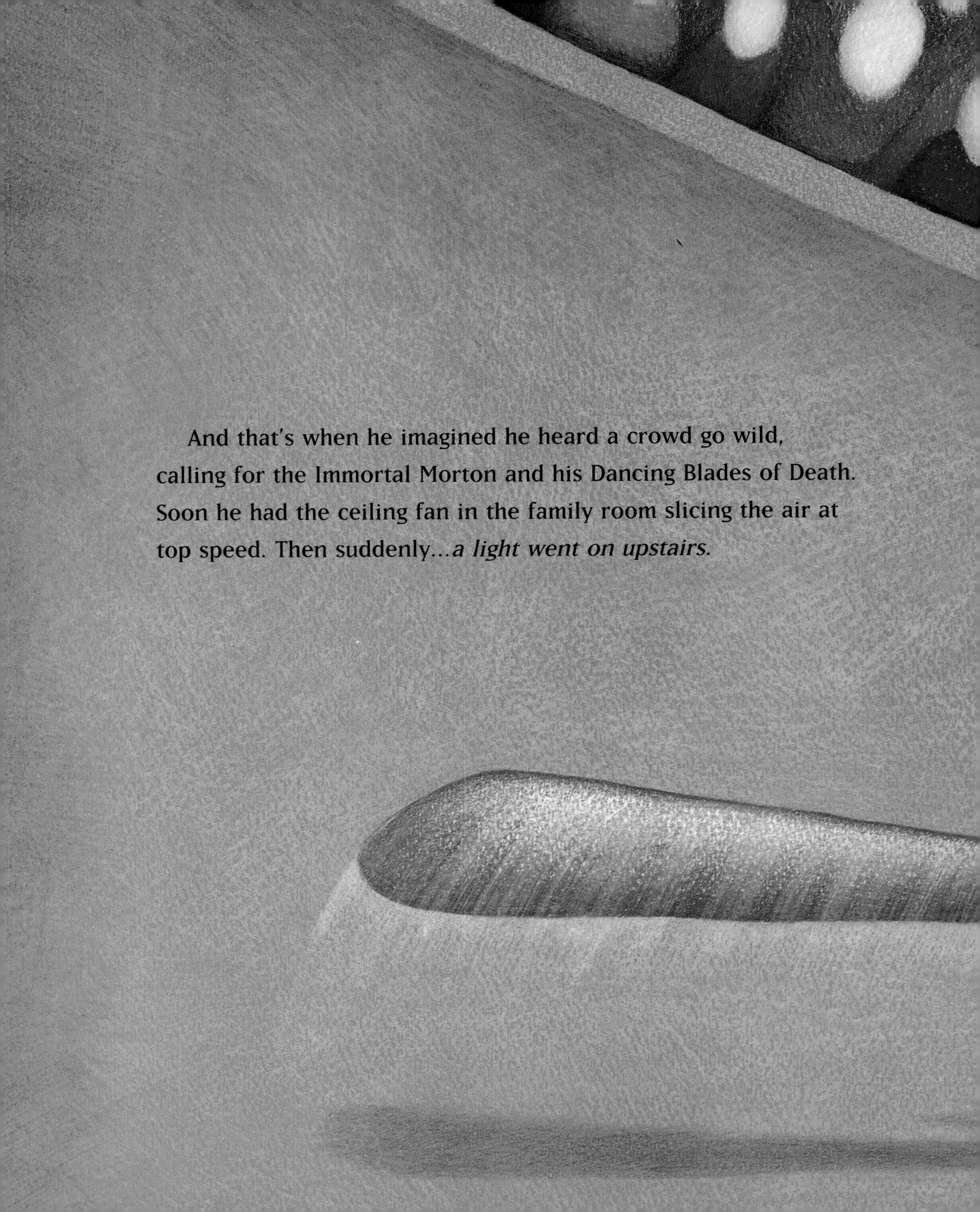

And that's when he imagined he heard a crowd go wild, calling for the Immortal Morton and his Dancing Blades of Death. Soon he had the ceiling fan in the family room slicing the air at top speed. Then suddenly...*a light went on upstairs.*

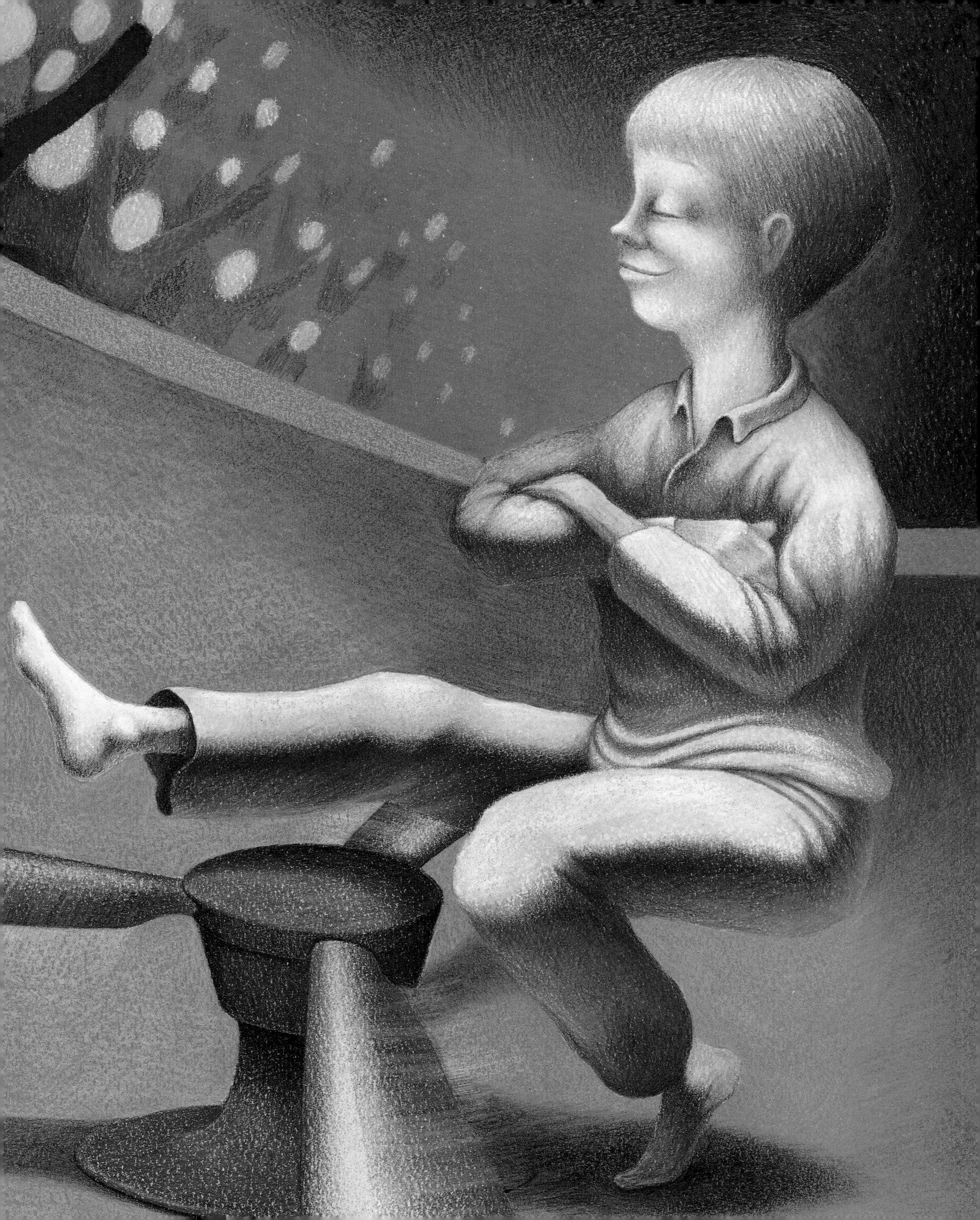

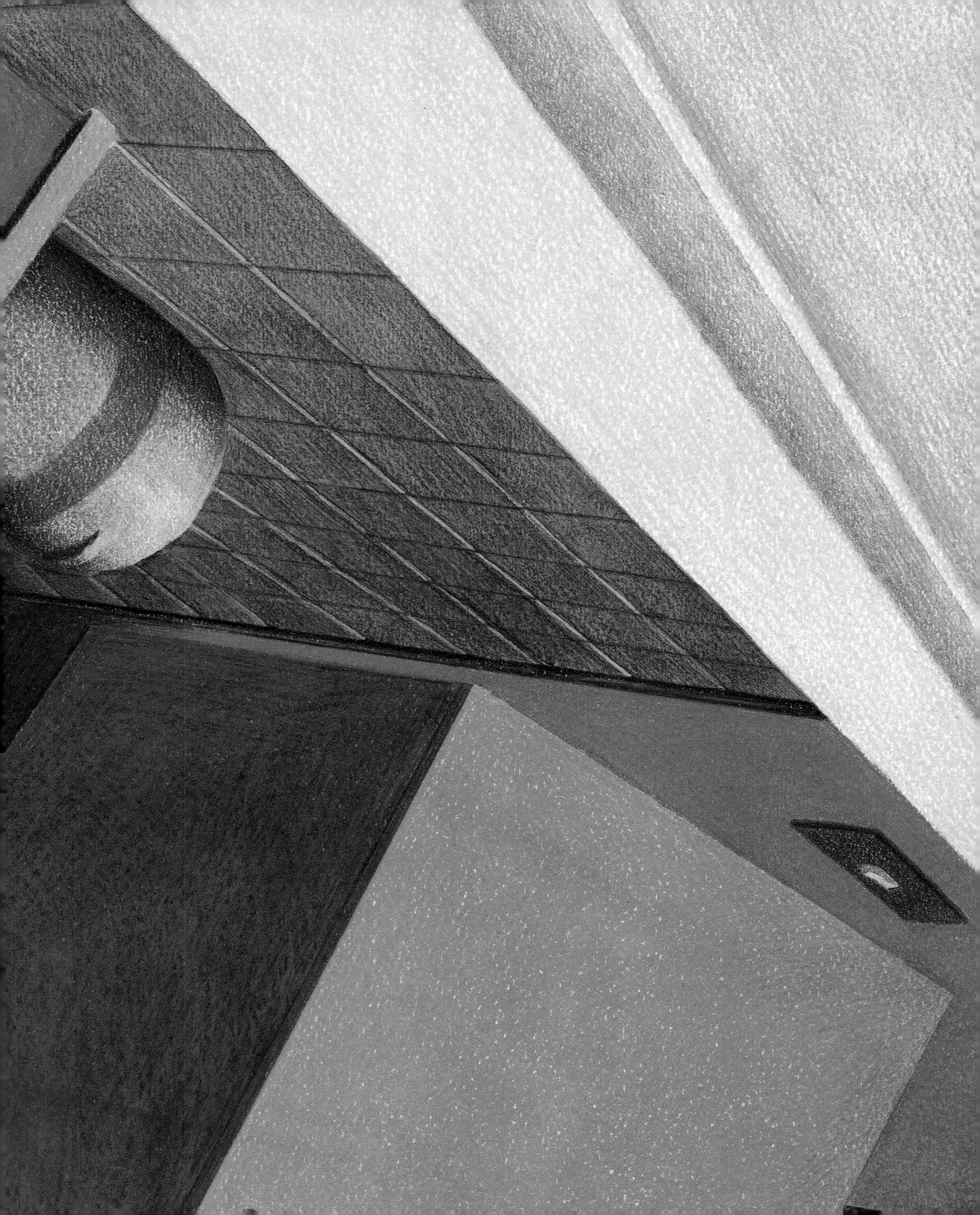

Quickly, Morton hopped into the dining room. He crouched behind the wall and peered out, trying not to breathe so he could hear better. Someone was coming!

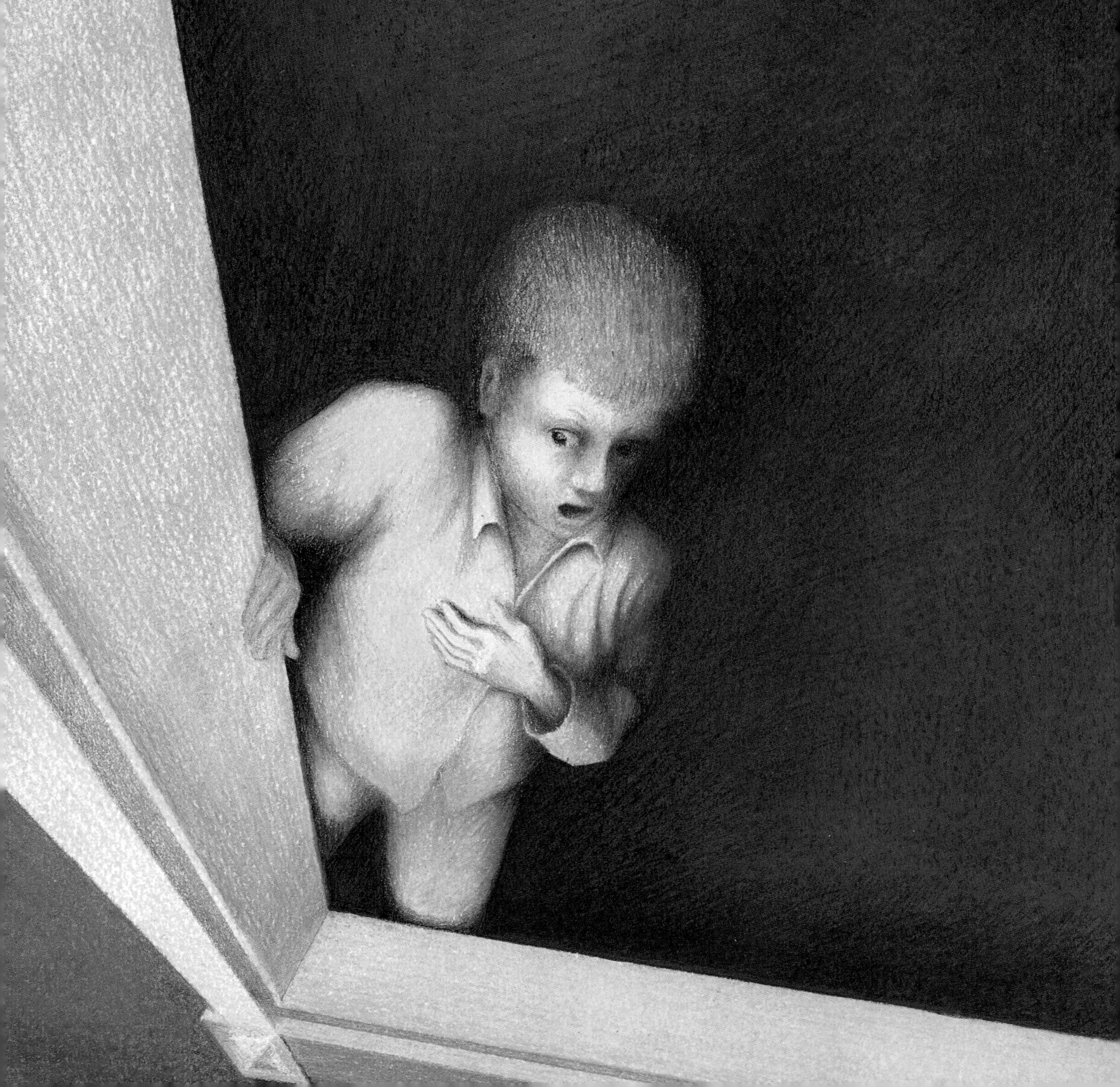

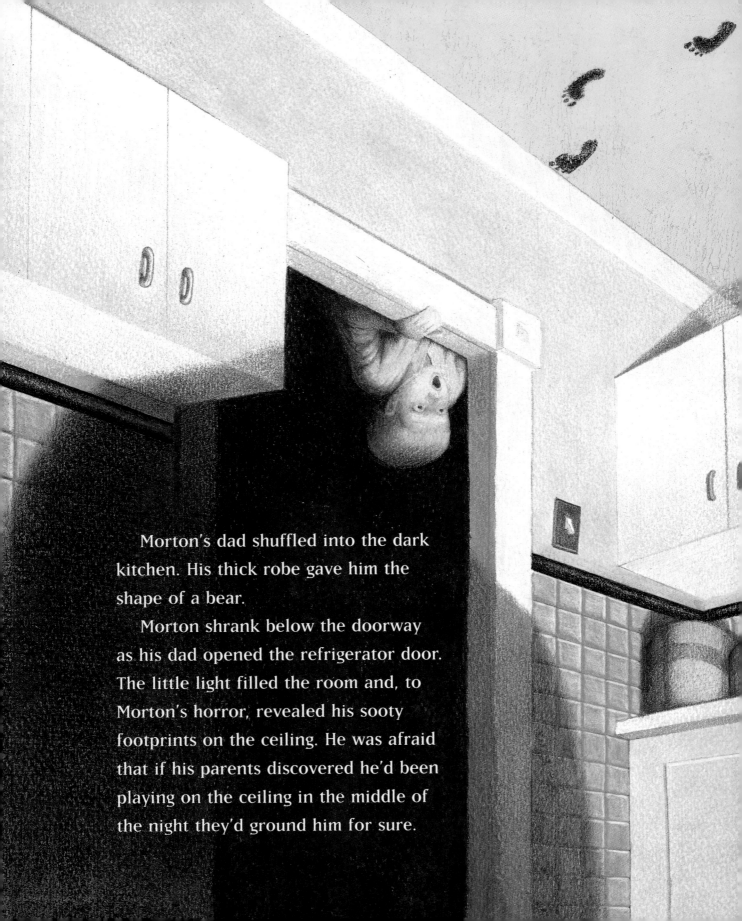

Morton's dad shuffled into the dark
kitchen. His thick robe gave him the
shape of a bear.

Morton shrank below the doorway
as his dad opened the refrigerator door.
The little light filled the room and, to
Morton's horror, revealed his sooty
footprints on the ceiling. He was afraid
that if his parents discovered he'd been
playing on the ceiling in the middle of
the night they'd ground him for sure.

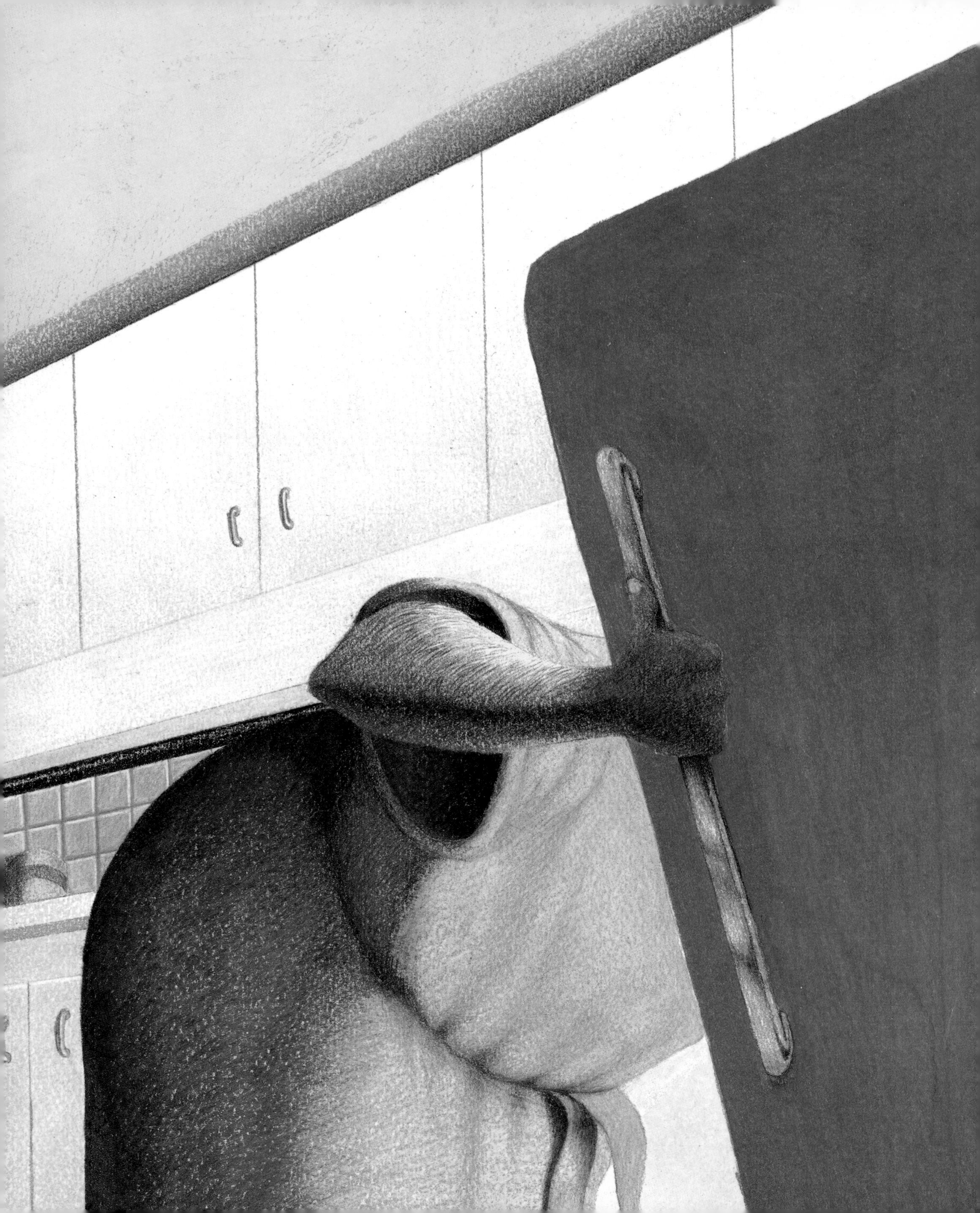

Morton's dad found some orange juice and drank
it from the pitcher, even though the rule in Morton's
house was that you were supposed to use a glass. Of
course, having broken the law of gravity, Morton was
hardly in a position to say anything.

Morton's dad put the empty pitcher back in the
refrigerator without looking up. He stumbled out of
the kitchen like a bald-headed bear going to sleep for
the winter. He never saw his son or the footprints
above his head.

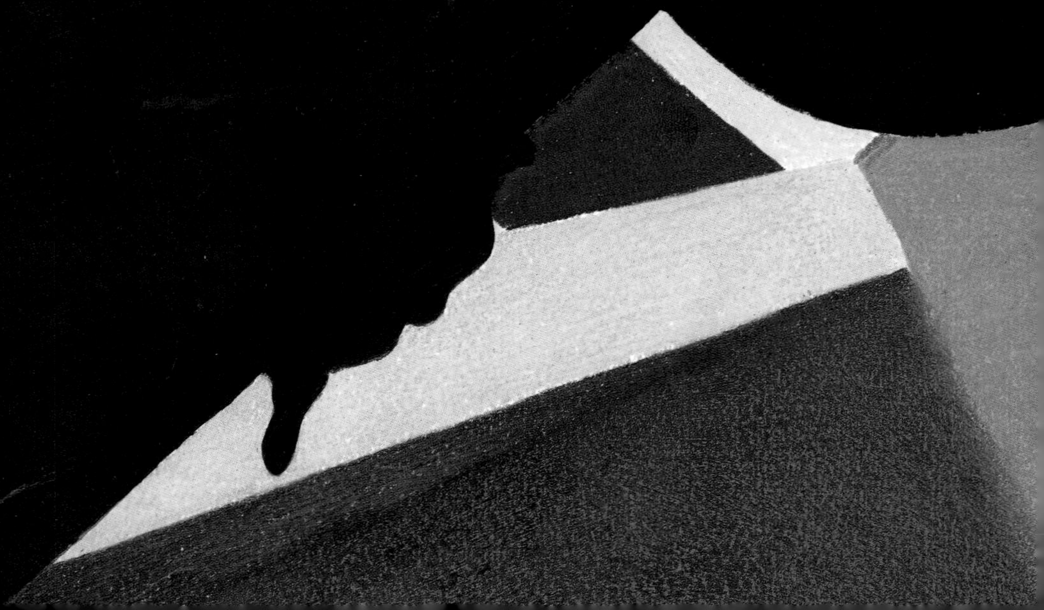

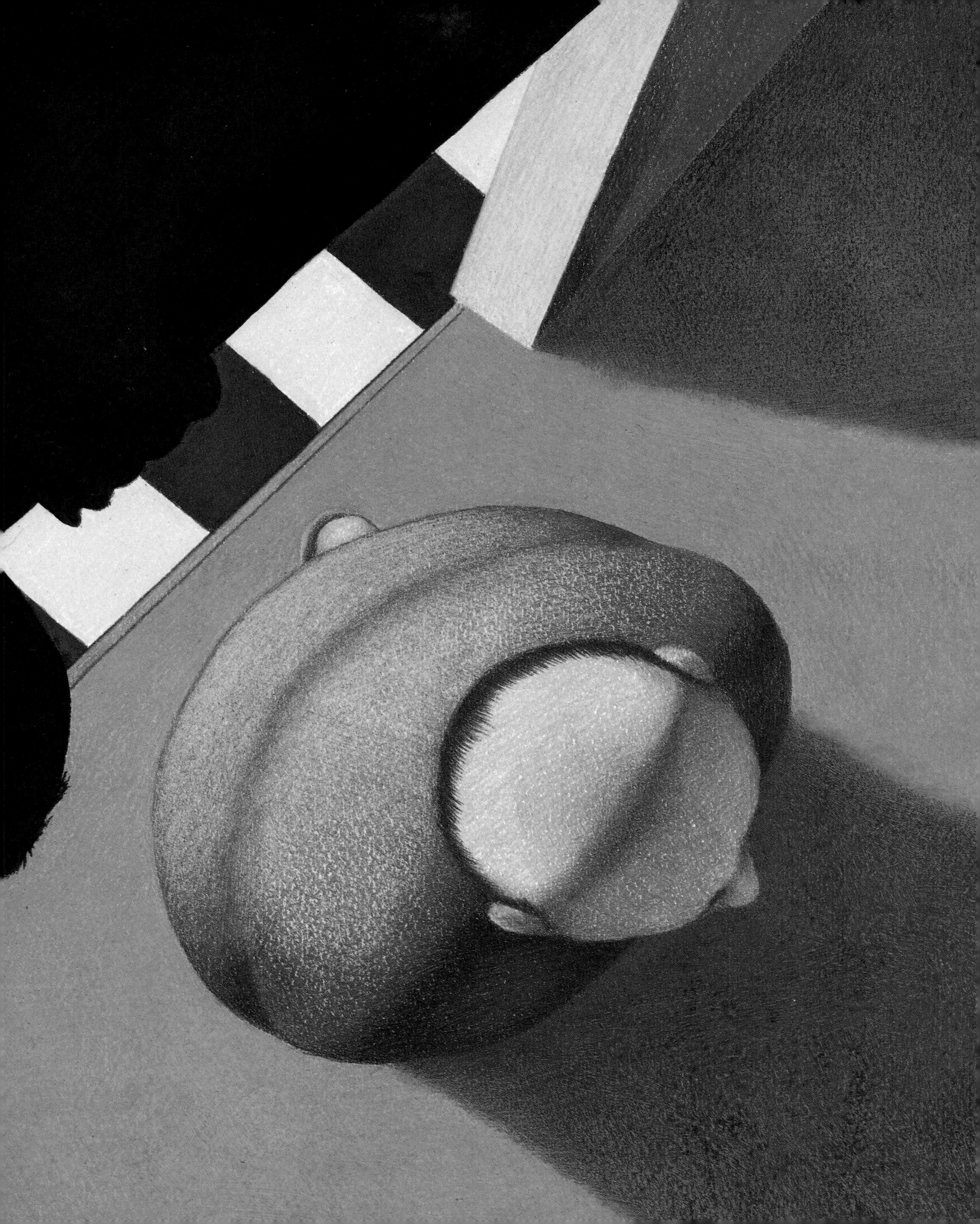

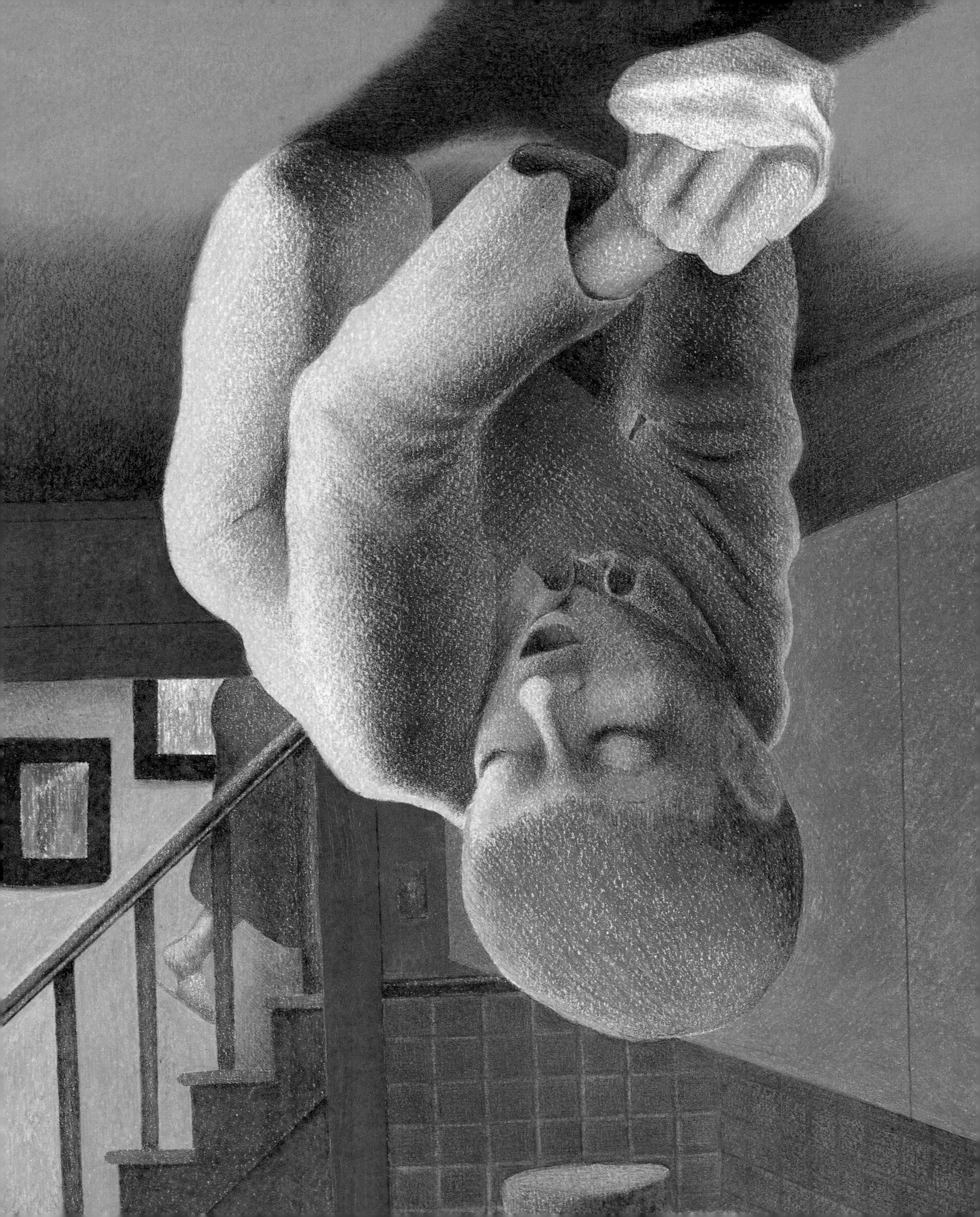

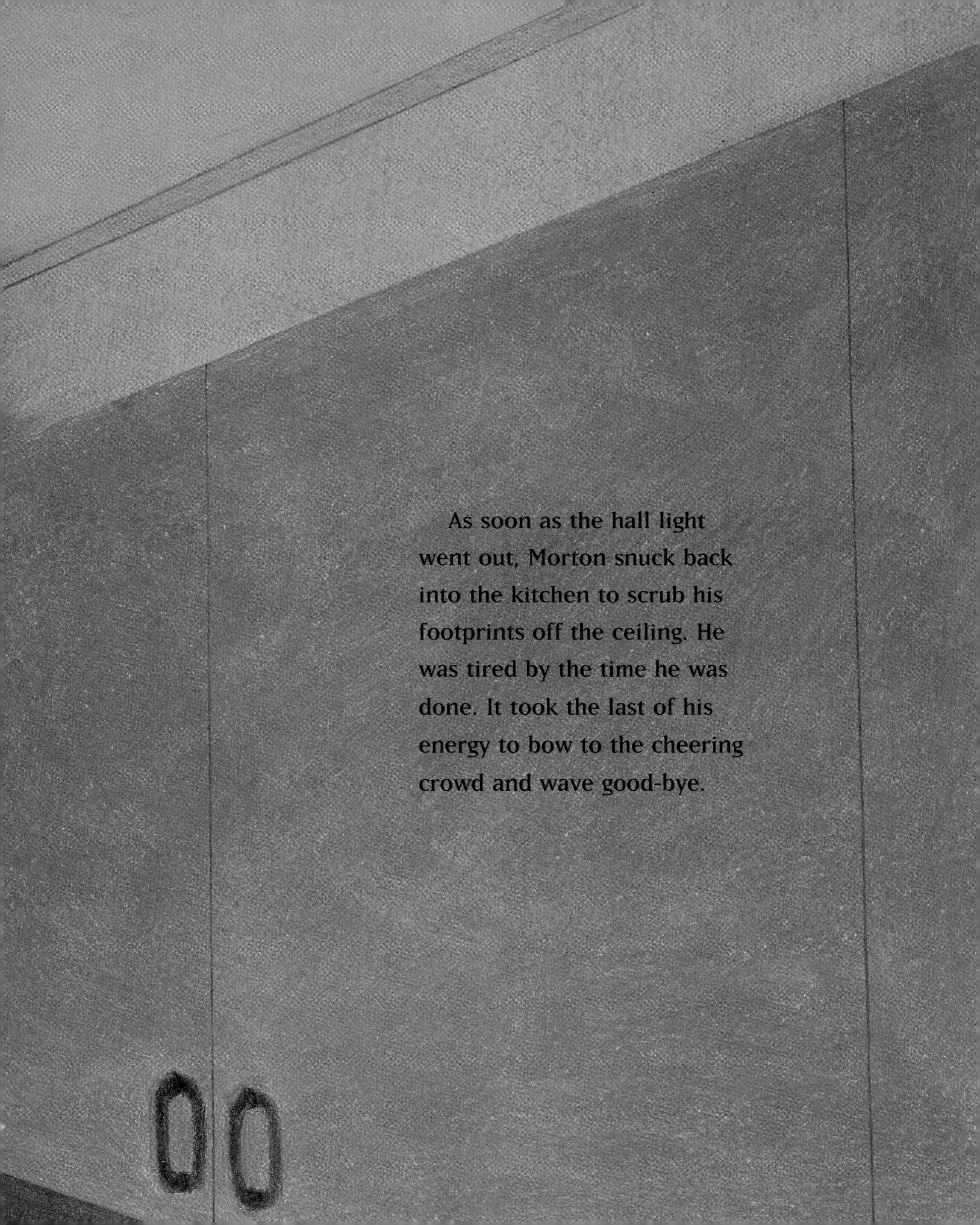

As soon as the hall light went out, Morton snuck back into the kitchen to scrub his footprints off the ceiling. He was tired by the time he was done. It took the last of his energy to bow to the cheering crowd and wave good-bye.

In the upstairs hall Morton paused outside the room that used to be his to listen to his sisters snoring softly like jungle cats. He made faces at the girls just because he felt like it, knowing they couldn't tattle. Then he climbed wearily into his new room.

He had already decided he wouldn't say a word about waking upside down. That way nobody could tell him not to do it any more. Or make him let his little sisters tag along.

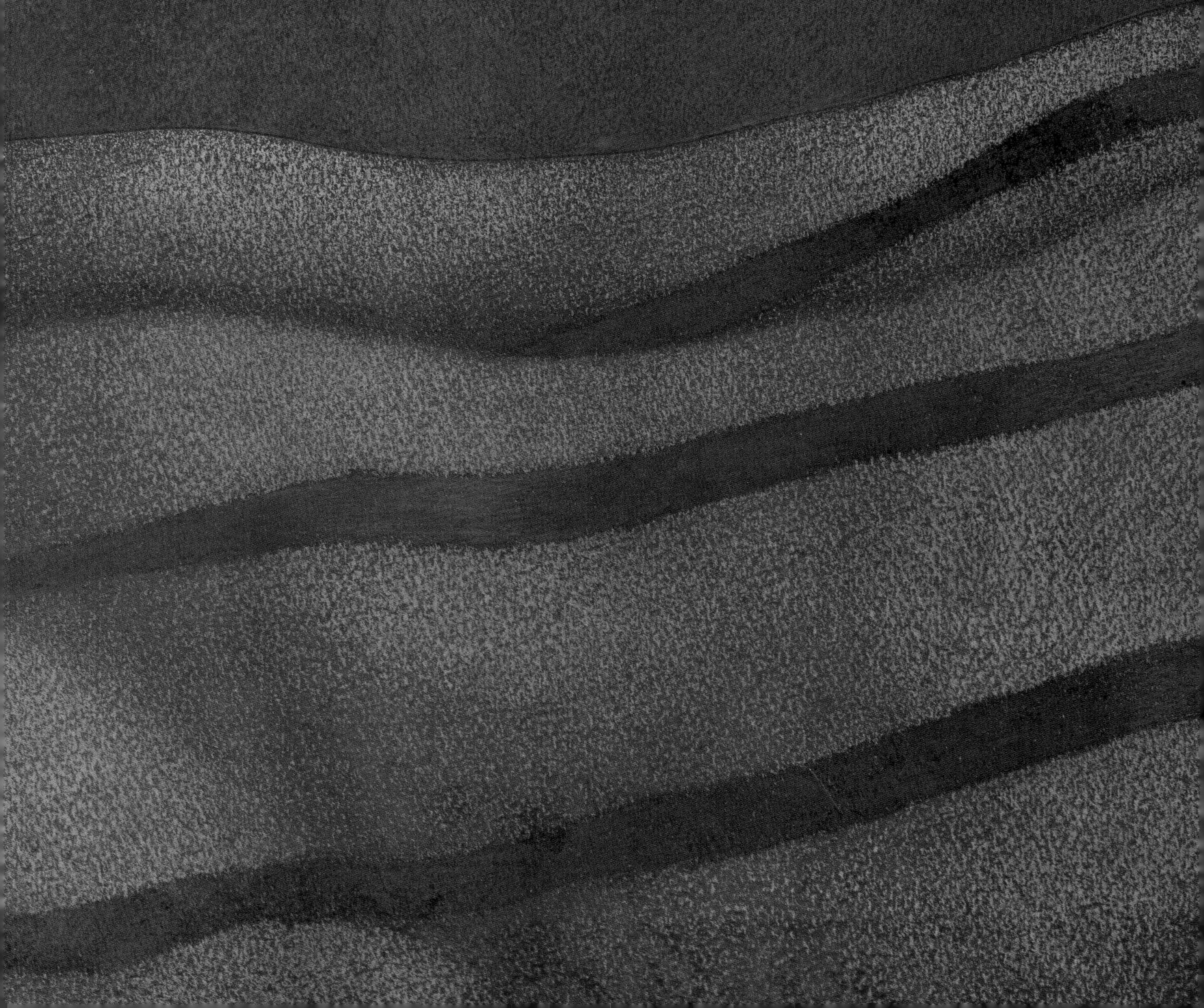

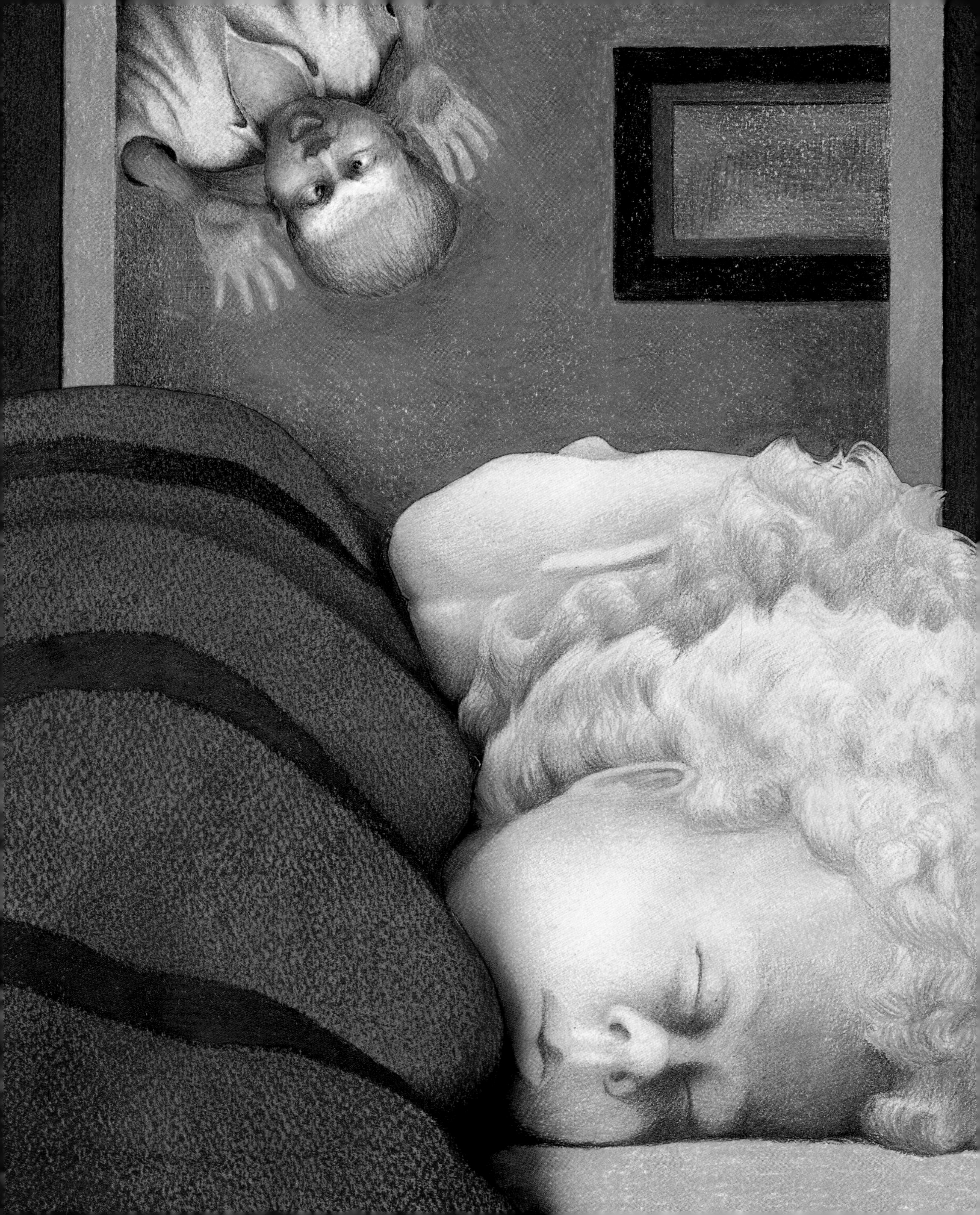

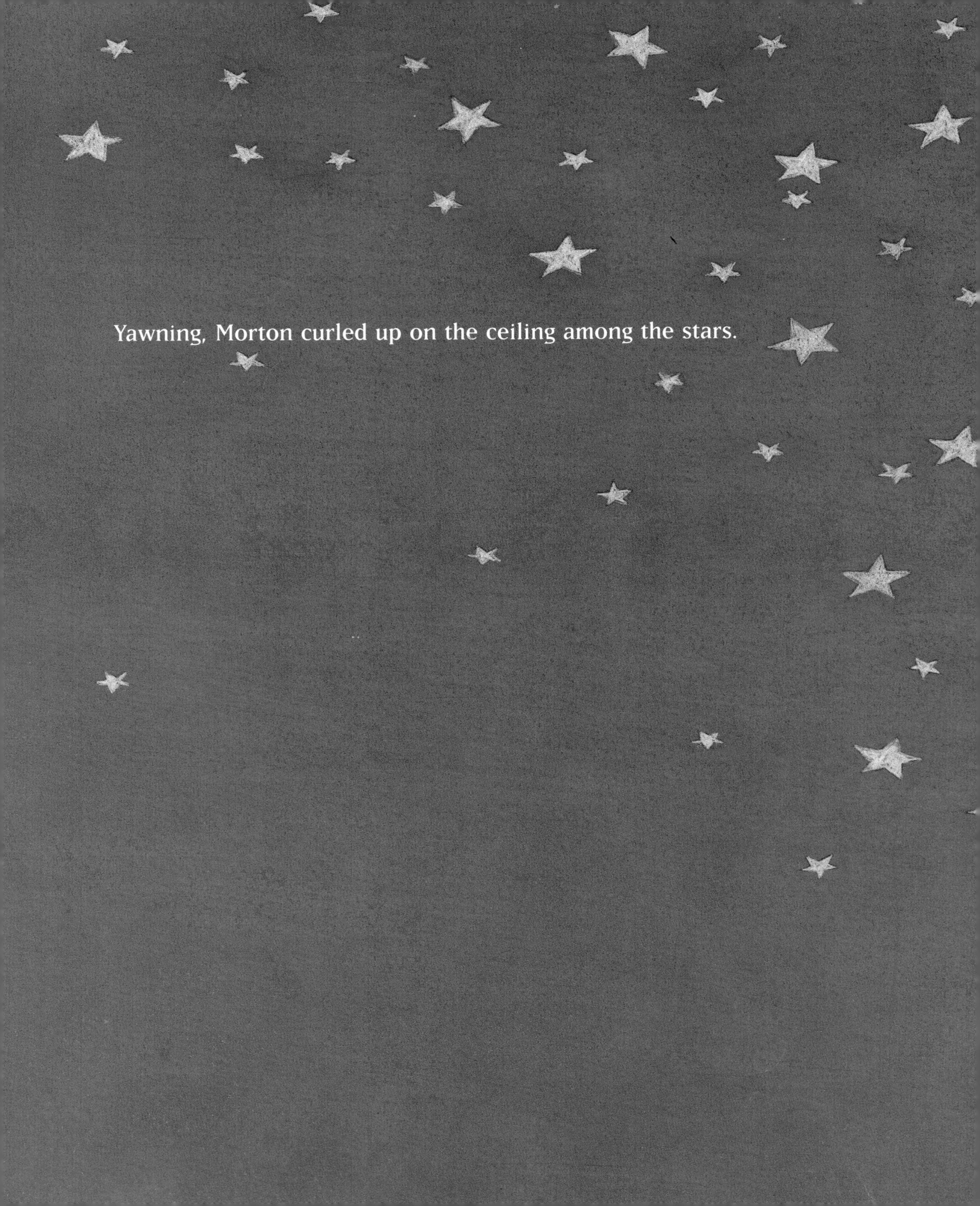

Yawning, Morton curled up on the ceiling among the stars.

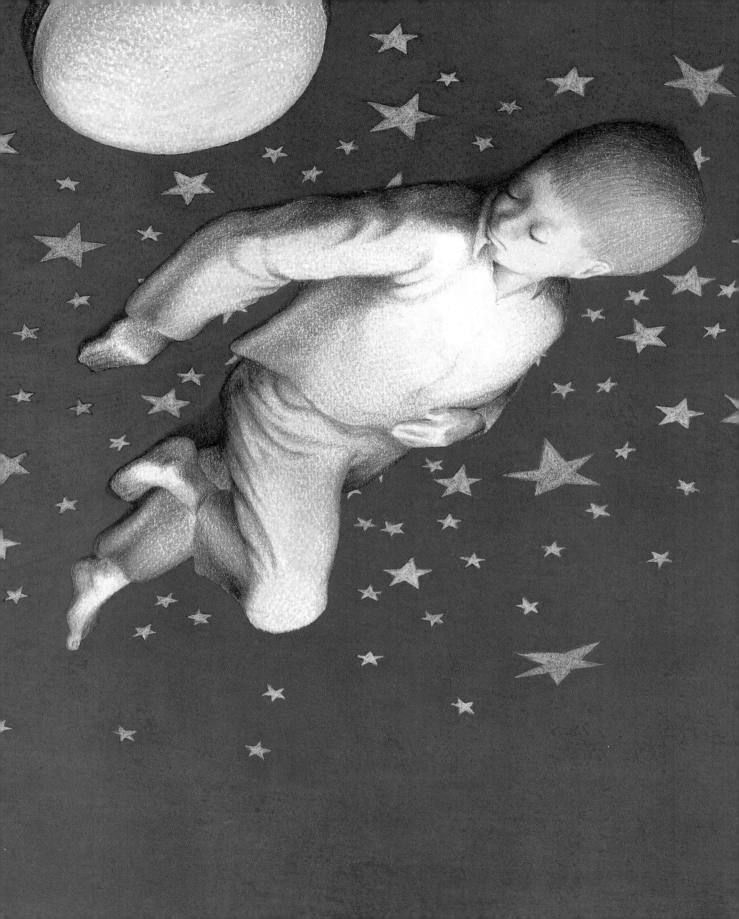

When he woke up the next morning,
he was back in bed, right where everyone
expected him to be. Except that now he
was smiling.

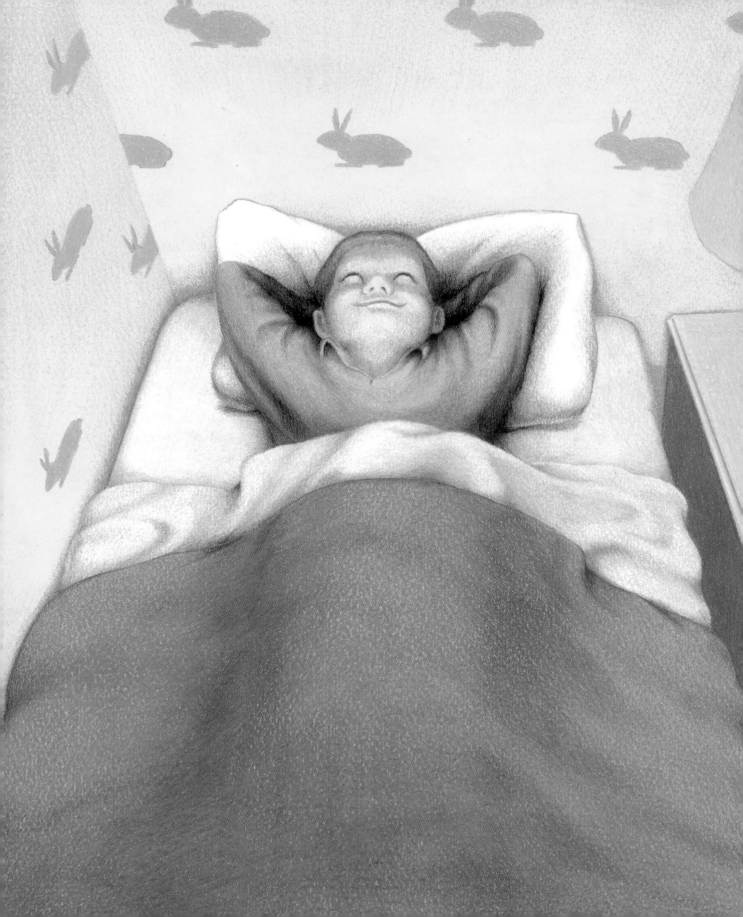